KV-684-925

The
Last Act

After studying Fine Art for a while, Laura Ellen Kennedy went to university in London (reading Philosophy and the History of Art at UCL). Working in a bookshop until she got her first job in journalism, she then wrote for women's and teen magazines for several years. She now works for a children's charity in London and lives in Hertfordshire with her husband.

The
Last Act

LAURA ELLEN KENNEDY

PICCADILLY PRESS • LONDON

For my parents,
for their unwavering love and support.

First published in Great Britain in 2009
by Piccadilly Press Ltd,
5 Castle Road, London NW1 8PR
www.piccadillypress.co.uk

Text copyright © Laura Ellen Kennedy, 2009

All rights reserved. No part of this publication may be
reproduced, stored in a retrieval system, or transmitted in any
form or by any means, electronic, mechanical, photocopying,
recording or otherwise, without the prior
permission of the copyright owner.

The right of Laura Ellen Kennedy to be identified as Author of
this work has been asserted by her in accordance with the
Copyright, Designs and Patents Act 1988

A catalogue record for this book is available
from the British Library

ISBN: 978 1 85340 013 6 (paperback)

1 3 5 7 9 10 8 6 4 2

Printed in the UK by CPI Bookmarque, Croydon, CR0 4TD
Cover design by Patrick Knowles
Cover photo: © Roy Bishop/Trevillion

© **Mixed Sources**
Product group from well-managed
forests and other controlled sources
www.fsc.org Cert no. TT-COC-002227
FSC © 1996 Forest Stewardship Council

Chapter 1

I was still out of breath when I jumped on to the train, just in time. My hair was still damp and I noticed, once I was in the carriage and breathing normally, that my jumper was inside out.

As I sidled though the carriage in search of somewhere to sit, I also couldn't help noticing that Jade and Jenni (Year Twelve's very own Devil Duo) had bagged their usual seats together, no doubt by elbowing past anyone so unlucky as to be standing in the way. They were staring at me with their upper lips curled up to their nostrils.

'Oh my God, she's such a disgusting mess. Hasn't she ever heard of a hairdryer?' Jenni 'whispered' so I could hear.

As I walked past, I made as if I was picking my nose, just to let her know I really couldn't care less if she thought

I was disgusting. As if I'd want my hair to look like hers, anyway. She clearly got up early every morning to torture it with electrical appliances and bully it into submission with goo and slime and yet, tragically, it still looked like a second-hand wig. Which had fallen into the toilet and been quickly wiped down with a dirty tea towel before being sent out to catch the 8.02 train. At least if my hair looked a bit like a haystack sometimes, I didn't have the embarrassment of everyone knowing I'd spent hours making it look that way.

I perched on the suitcase rack, keeping myself to myself, and pictured her, aged twenty-five, totally bald except for a few sticky wisps, sobbing in the doctor's office, being told it was all down to over-use of her beloved straighteners . . .

School that day was, as usual, OK, but pretty much just something to look forward to the end of. On Tuesday lunchtimes my friends Katie and Katy had badminton and I, being completely devoid of any sporting ability, had lunch by myself. On this particular Tuesday, I had to go into town to replace the sandwich I'd carefully made for myself and then left in the fridge as I'd rushed out of the door that morning.

I bought a stand-in and found a bench to sit on by the church, away from the shopping centre where Jade and Jenni and all their self-obsessed friends hang out. I rummaged for the local newspaper in my bag and searched through for the article about the theatre that my dad had told me to read. For some reason I felt my heart start to thump quite fast as I read it.

Dad had been looking at the paper over toast that morning as I'd lifted my sleep-filled arm to pour my coffee, trying to get my eyes to come to terms with the fact I was awake and I needed them to stay open.

There was an ear-splitting clink as Dad put his mug down without looking and caught the edge of his plate. If he'd noticed, he did a great impression of someone who hadn't, cheerfully turning the page of his newspaper without a thought for my eardrums.

'Hey Zoë, look at this – they've got a lottery grant to do up the old Hemingford Theatre – you know, the one near the library that's all dark and boarded up? That's great news! It's a lovely building. They're looking for actors to be in their opening plays – look!'

Dad's a morning person, in case you hadn't guessed. And today, on top of this, he was in one of his excitable moods. As I'd swayed over to the breakfast bar bearing my hot mug of caffeinated elixir in one hand, rubbing my determinedly unconscious face with the other, I marvelled at his ability to be so perky so early.

'Dad, I'm not an actor – yet. Anyway, they don't want schoolgirls for their play; they don't mean me.'

'No, no, they do, Zo – read it.' He practically shoved the paper into my face, and he wasn't having it when I grimaced and batted him away. He was like a puppy or something, yapping and jumping around your feet, making you happy and annoyed at the same time.

People say he's an eccentric – and that it's only right, because he's a lecturer. They love it when they can put you neatly into a pigeon-hole like that. They conveniently overlook the fact he just teaches media studies at a further education college, not English literature at Cambridge or Oxford or somewhere like that. He can be so ditzy sometimes, he makes me feel like I'm the adult – anything involving coordination or memory stumps him. Some days it's hilarious. Some days, not so much.

'It's a youth project thingy, a lot of different short plays – all different ages and experience – for an opening showcase. There are auditions soon, in a couple of weeks I think it said. You should go along. You'd be great.' He jumped up and grabbed his coat from the hallway, pulling it on with half a piece of peanut-buttered toast still in his hand.

'Promise me you'll read it, and log on to the site and have a look, OK? It sounds like an opportunity.'

I stared, imagining the greasy streaks he'd probably just made on the inside of his coat sleeve, and just nodded and mmhmmed. He waved goodbye, grabbed his briefcase and disappeared through the back door.

I figured I'd read the paper on the train. I dropped it by my bag as I took my coffee and slumped through into the living room to turn on the TV. I had to concentrate on averting my eyes from the hall mirror then, because I could feel my hair was sticking up in stupid, pillow-sculpted clumps, which I really did not need to see.

I knew full well, as I put on morning TV and let myself get sucked into watching it, that I'd end up leaving it till the last minute to get in the shower. I knew I'd probably end up having to run to get the train again, but I let myself watch anyway. And sure enough, I was legging it through the front door twenty minutes later, forgetting my lunch. At least I managed to keep my promise to Dad, grabbing the newspaper on my way out and stuffing it into my bag as I ran to the station. Mornings never get any easier.

Sitting in the grey daylight by the church, absorbed in my own quiet little space, reading about the theatre, I felt all this unexpected excitement tingling in me. Drama was the only thing at school I really enjoyed and felt like I was good at. Those lessons were the only time I felt like I could let out all the stuff that was bottled up in me. I could be outspoken or glamorous, or anything else just as out of character, and it didn't matter because it wasn't really me – I was acting. Thinking I might get the chance to perform properly, in a real production in a real theatre instead of just a school play, made me buzz with anticipation.

The school plays I'd been in were fun but always felt a bit half-hearted. Plus there was always the same politics with the casting, with the same people always fighting over the best parts, not because they really wanted them but because they thought they ought to be first choice. It'd always be someone from Jade and Jenni's pack that got them because they made the most fuss about it, or Minnie and Clara because they were the prettiest and thinnest. If I could escape all those cliques and pigeon-holes and really just act . . .

A sudden, cold breeze brought me out of my thoughts and when I looked at my mobile to check the time, I realised it was too late to look at the theatre website before afternoon lessons. I'd have to rush to even get to class in time. So I had to wait till my last lesson was over and rush home to beat Dad to the computer. It didn't take me long to find the page about the youth theatre projects and the audition times. As I wrote down all the details of the auditions, I had to tell myself not to get too excited too soon.

I figured if I let my expectations get too high, I'd only be disappointed. And I've been through enough disappointment in my time to know it's worth making an effort to avoid. Nothing's more disappointing than having your mum go off and leave you when you're too young to understand why. That might sound like a weird way to describe it, 'disappointing', like it's just a bit of an understatement. And I suppose I'm being a bit sarcastic, or ironic or whatever, like I'm often told I am, but real, deep disappointment can cut you right to your core. I was so little when she left, I didn't understand then. I never really believed it was for good. I imagined she'd just gone out, like she had so many times before, and she'd be back again soon. The truth didn't hit me in a big, devastating wave. It hit me in little bits, over and over again. Each bit of proof I was wrong was like a vicious little piece of the painful truth coming out. Every time there was an unexpected knock at the door and it wasn't her. Every time the post came on birthdays or holidays, or when I'd passed an exam or won a prize, and there was no card – no letter to say she was proud. Every time I came down for breakfast and she wasn't sitting at the kitchen table, holding Dad's hand, explaining why she'd had to go, admitting it was a mistake, saying sorry. My heart would split open at the bottom and hope would drop out of it. X = the grand sum of a million and one small but utterly crushing disappointments.

Not that I'm angling for sympathy. I know feeling sorry for yourself shouldn't win you any prizes, I'm just explaining why I didn't want to feel the excitement I was feeling. I just wanted to be able to be positive without getting too emotional before I knew if I had a chance, that's all.

The auditions would be mostly 'cold readings', the site said. Yikes, that meant having some play you'd never seen before thrust into your hand and having to just be brilliant on the spot. No pressure then. And, just to add to the cringe factor, it said if you were going for musical parts you should prepare a song and bring sheet music! Now I'm not

7

big on musicals, but what if there was something with singing that sounded really good on the day? I couldn't rule myself out.

I felt like someone had just nudged a big red panic button on the back of my head. I only had one weekend and one week of evenings to get ready. Why couldn't they do them the weekend *after* half-term instead of the one before? I grabbed my diary and started blocking out chunks of time to concentrate on preparing, like it was a revision timetable (only one I actually expected to stick to).

That week, I spent every spare minute picking up plays from Dad's shelves and reading out random passages. Lovely Katie came over one evening and was my audience-of-one and prompter. I got hold of some sheet music for musicals I knew, so I could practise the songs without having to rely on my very sketchy music-reading skills. I think Dad was surprised at how much work I was doing. Instead of watching TV or sitting at the computer, I was in my room, singing or monologuing into my mirror. Every couple of hours, Dad would knock on the door, give me a grin, a thumbs-up or a cup of tea and then scurry off again. I think he was just happy to have the living room to himself, but I felt good that he seemed so pleased I was putting the effort in.

School almost got more bearable that week, just because I had something to look forward to that no one else knew about. My secret was like a shield I could use in the corridors – when the Katies weren't around and I had to dodge nasty comments from Jade and Jenni's lot on my own, it felt like it mattered a little bit less.

I'm not sure any amount of practice could have prepared me for arriving on the actual day, though. When I got out of the car that Saturday and saw people everywhere, I was hit by the overwhelming noise. Swarms of people chatted nervously and excitedly outside – some people seemed to be in huddles with teachers or coaches, some were even limbering up their singing voices right there in the street. These were all people I'd be competing with. And, worse, I spotted some people from school, Laurel and Fi, two of Jade's mates, 'singing' and flicking their hair about.

I was frozen to the spot while my heart and soul were already making their escape, sprinting away down the street. I was standing there, just where I'd stepped out of the car, clutching the door with my left hand like it was a protective force field, my knuckles whitening. And then Dad read my mind. He leaned over from the driver's side and found my other hand. Coming out of my trance, I leaned back into the car. He was smiling, softly and seriously as he squeezed my little-girl hand tightly in his big dad hand.

'You can do it,' he said.

Chapter 2

I put on my best 'focused' face and headed straight for the entrance, paying as little attention to the crowds of people as I could. I felt shaky all over, but I was going to do this and Dad was going to be proud of me.

Looking around reception for a noticeboard or something with some kind of instruction, or a list of audition times or productions – anything, I saw a girl sitting alone on a row of chairs by the windows. She was looking as nervous as I felt, bent over a script, chewing her thumbnail and jiggling her feet. It surprised me how easy it was for me to go over and speak to her; I'd usually be more shy about that stuff.

'Hi. Do you mind if I sit here?' I asked.

She looked up at me and smiled. Her eyes looked sort of restless and wild but somehow still really friendly. 'Mmhmm,' she said, nodding and then looking back down at her page. That confused me.

'You do?'

'Oh! No! Sorry, I mean go ahead.' She let out a nervy giggle and waved at the chairs next to her with her script. 'Sorry. Brain scramble.'

'I know what you mean,' I offered as I sat down. 'I'm so nervous. I feel like I'm getting exam results or something.'

'Oh my God. Me too.' She virtually spun in her chair to face me and then pressed her hand to the top of her head as if she thought her brain might pop out of there. 'Sooo nervous. I just hate thinking I'm going to have people watching me and judging me – which is basically what auditions *are*, so I really don't know what I'm doing here!'

She made such a hilarious face then – a sort of crazed mixture of quizzical panic and wonder – that I burst out laughing. Thankfully, instead of taking it the wrong way, she laughed too. I decided right away that she was brilliant.

'Urrrrgh,' she said, 'I wish they'd hurry up with the lists and stuff. I asked a woman on the desk there, who seems to have disappeared now, where all the information was and she said they were bringing it all out on boards in about five or ten minutes. That was fifteen minutes ago. I mean. Come. On . . . Oh, I'm Gemma, by the way.'

'Hi. Zoë.' I smiled.

It was another ten minutes before the boards finally emerged and Gemma and I chatted easily while we waited. She sort of looked like a doll. She was small with shiny,

11

almost-black hair, poker straight, with a perfect, neat fringe, porcelain-white skin and huge, round, turquoise eyes. Her subtle, perfectly neat black eyeliner framed just the tops of her eyes and flicked daintily at the outer edges. I wondered how she got it that perfect. But as surreally neat as she looked, she was totally chaotic when she spoke, and not the least bit prim or artificial. As reception started to fill up with all the people from outside, it already felt like I had a friend. She seemed much calmer for talking with me, and that made me feel less nervous too, which made so much difference when the hoards started to push and shove. It got harder and harder to read everything as we all gradually became one teetering heap of squashed bodies.

'Come over here.' Gemma grabbed my arm and pulled me out of the herd. She had a notebook and beckoned me over to sit with her on some steps where it was quieter. 'I've copied all the times and stuff down – come and have a look at what you want to do.' We huddled round her notes and made our plans together. There were six auditions I wanted to go to and Gemma picked five. We arranged to meet back in reception for lunch and said we'd meet up again at five-thirty when we'd both be done.

My first audition was horrible. It was for this play about a dinner party, and the woman holding the session was terrifying. You had to queue outside the room, and you got to see a bit of the script and character descriptions while you waited, so you could see which parts you wanted to go for. But when I told this woman which part I wanted to try, she was like, 'Oh, no dear, I don't think you're right for that,' and she made this sharp, pointy face, which I think was supposed to be a smile but was about as pleasant as having your foot stamped on by someone in kitten heels. She made me read this other part and then as I read the lines she kept interrupting me to tell me to do it a different way. Which doesn't exactly build your confidence.

That made me not want to do the next one, especially as it was for a musical part in *The Wizard of Oz* and I was extra nervous about singing. But actually the woman taking that one was really lovely and made me feel relaxed as soon as I went in.

After that, I loved the rest of the day, even though I was in a state of nervousness pretty much the whole time. When I met Gemma for lunch she was literally jumping with excitement. I had to practically hold her still just to try and calm her down enough so we could go to the supermarket to get something to eat. It was so funny.

'I can't eat anything. I'm too nervous!' she said.

'I know what you mean,' I replied, 'but you should try, honestly, or at least have a sugary drink or something. With the amount of nervous energy you're using up, you'll pass out this afternoon otherwise.'

'You're right,' she resolved. 'I'm glad you're here to be my voice of reason, Zoë. It doesn't seem like I have my own one of those.'

After lunch we wished each other luck and went off in different directions for the afternoon session. When we met again at the end though, we realised we'd tried out for the same part in one of the plays.

'Oh no! I can't be friends with you any more – we're rivals!' cried Gemma when we realised. I didn't know her that well yet but decided to go with my gut instinct and assume she was joking.

'Ha ha. It's true – I bet a lot of people went for that part though – it's a cool play, sort of dark, being a murder story and a sort of comedy in one.'

'Well, let's hope one of us gets it . . . even if it's you!' Gemma grinned. 'I'd better give you my number, so if you "get the call" you can tell me and put me out of my misery.' She rummaged in her bag for her mobile and we swapped numbers.

She walked with me over to the cinema, where Dad had said he'd pick me up, because it was on her way to the station, and then we said goodbye. While I waited, I felt half tensely impatient, wondering if I'd get a part, and half happily tired, thinking that even if I didn't, maybe I'd made a friend. I didn't mind having to wait a quarter of an hour for Dad to turn up (he misremembered our arrangement, of course). He made up for it by letting me yammer on about the day all the way home. And through dinner.

The ring of the telephone woke me up the next morning at

about ten-thirty. While I was coming round, Dad answered. There was a bit of mumbling and then I heard him say, 'Ahh, that's great news! Brilliant, I'll let her know and get her to call you . . .'

I scrambled out of bed and, as I got to the bottom of the stairs, he was just putting the phone down and scribbling a note.

'That was *The Wizard of Oz*. You're second senior munchkin,' he announced, looking up from the pad.

I got a little rush of excitement, knowing I was in – that whatever happened I could be involved in one of the productions. But, although I knew there'd be loads of people who went for roles and didn't get any offers, I felt a little bit disappointed too. I'd read for the good witch and even a speaking munchkin wasn't quite as good.

'What do you think?' Dad looked over the top of his glasses at me, clearly trying to work out what my expression meant.

'Yeah, that's really good . . .' I started.

'But not what you really wanted?' he guessed.

'It's a part though. I didn't know if I'd get offered anything, so it's really good.'

'Well, you got one offer, maybe you'll get more. Don't decide anything yet – I'll be your manager for the day, eh? Answer all the calls for you and then you can weigh up the offers tonight?' He clapped his hands and then rubbed them together all businesslike.

I grinned at his optimism and nodded OK, not expecting him to be exactly rushed off his feet with that job. But, actually, by three-thrity, I had a decision to make after all – although it was an easy one.

'Ha! Oh my God!' I jumped off the sofa when Dad told me I'd got a part in the murder comedy play. It wasn't the part Gemma and I had both gone for, but it was the other female lead. I was so happy. And terrified. I suddenly wondered if I'd actually be able to do it. Then I thought how brilliant it would be. Then, I finally realised that, just maybe, that meant Gemma had got the other part. Then we could be in it together. That would be so perfect. Spookily enough, that's when my mobile rang . . .

The squeals nearly deafened me when I told Gemma I'd got the part of Rebecca. And I allowed myself my own squeal or two when she said she got picked too, for the part we'd both read for. It all seemed too good to be true. And Gemma's hyperactive chatter kept me distracted from my nerves.

'Did they tell you when rehearsals were starting? I was too excited to listen properly . . . Hey,' she interrupted herself, not giving me a chance to answer, 'what do you think our leading man will be like?'

Chapter 3

In the third act, I got shot. Then dragged off and locked in the cellar. I couldn't wait.

I had the full script in front of me – the director, Steve, had emailed it to us in advance so we could read through properly before the first practice. I thought I couldn't be any more excited about getting started until I sat down in the kitchen to read that printout. I was so ready to get on with it that I couldn't keep still. *Foul Play* read the curly type on the front page. I practically tore open the cover like the wrapping off a present. It was like being a little kid at Christmas. Of course, if I was that excited, I knew Gemma would be about ready to explode. I figured I'd give her a call when I'd finished reading.

My character, Rebecca, was newly-wedded to Tristan (how weird to be playing a wife!) and was an heiress who ran her dead father's shipping business (it was set in the Fifties so it was quite cool, ahead-of-its-time in the feminism department, to be playing a business woman). But while Rebecca is away on business trips, Tristan starts an affair with a 'shop-girl' (not so feminist, in the terminology department) called Diana – that was Gemma's part.

Of course, Rebecca, being pretty smart, knows just what's going on and fakes a business trip so she can walk in on her new husband doing the dirty on her. Only, Tristan panics when she catches him with Diana, grabs a gun from the sideboard drawer, and shoots Rebecca. Diana isn't keen on the whole violence thing, but goes along with it because she wants to protect Tristan, and the panicked lovers lock Rebecca's body in the cellar while they decide what to do. Only it turns out Rebecca isn't quite dead, so while the nervy couple are frantically planning how to cover up their murder, not realising there hasn't actually been one, yet, Rebecca is causing trouble in the basement . . .

Before I could finish reading, my phone rang. You guessed it, it was Gemma, calling to screech in my ear. When she'd chilled out a bit, i.e. *ages* later, we read some lines together over the phone.

'I wish we had more scenes *together*,' Gemma said.

'Me too, but you can kind of see why we don't – it's understandable, what with the whole love-rivalry, murder-plot thing . . .'

'I guess so,' Gemma sighed. 'I'll be the man for you in scene one then, and you can be mine in two.' She put on a deep voice and read Tristan's part, which made it hard for me to concentrate on my lines.

'*Gemma*, you're making me laugh too much,' I said, giving up. 'I can't wait to meet the others . . .'

'Oooh, me neither. Now, I've been thinking a lot about who we'll get for our Tristan. He'll be hot, hopefully. And single.'

'I can go along with that, I reckon. Not too hot, though, I'll need to keep my mind on the job.'

'But it wouldn't be any good if he minged, would it? I mean, it'd make us look bad, given that we're basically fighting over him in the play.'

'Good point,' I said, glancing at the calendar by the phone. 'Well, it's less than a week before we find out . . .'

'That's still too long!'

'Well, hello ladies,' said this cocky-looking guy, letting out a whistle of approval as he walked into the classroom at the college, that first rehearsal. 'Which one of you is my wife and which is my girlfriend? Cos I'm ready to get down to business.' He winked. Gemma and I exchanged looks.

'Yeah, and which one of you's gonna hurl first after that introduction – just so I know where to sit . . .' said the boy who came in next, quietly shutting the door behind them.

'Hello chaps, nice of you to join us.' Steve the director

looked at his watch and then through his eyebrows at the boys. 'Do sit down, please.'

Gemma and I shot each other another glance, eyebrows raised. I wondered what we'd let ourselves in for. The guys were about five minutes late – what would Steve be like if they were actually properly late, like a whole *ten* minutes? Plus, I wasn't sure about this boy with his bold attitude, walking straight in with his sexist flirting. He had a very charming, cheeky smile, but you could tell he used it to get away with stuff.

'Boys, this is Gemma, our Diana, and Zoë, who'll be playing Rebecca. Girls, this is Anton, who, you may have fathomed, will be playing Tristan, and our all-important everyman: butler, postman, locksmith and policeman, David.' He clapped his hands together. 'And now, let's get started, shall we – has everyone brought their scripts?'

I couldn't work out how old Steve was – he could have been anything from a stressed-out twenty-nine to a baby-faced forty-five. He wore a young-looking T-shirt and baggy jeans, but when he opened his mouth it was like an old woman talking. He was shortish, with dark blond, slightly wavy hair and a vaguely squidgy look. I don't mean he was fat, he just had a sort of slightly cuddly, teddy-bear feel to him, which is maybe why he felt the need to assert his authority so often, to compensate.

Anton was good-looking and certainly made the most of it. He sort of reminded me of Will Smith, in looks a bit but totally in his manner – that way of walking into a room, giving a million-dollar smile and completely taking over everyone's attention. David was more like a sort of smallish, blond, surferish Daniel Radcliffe and was much quieter.

I was always in awe of people like Anton, so full of confidence and so ready to speak. But I wasn't sure if it was a bit much, like he was a bit arrogant. But then just when he annoyed me, he'd make me laugh. Maybe I just resented that he pulled me in, totally. It was like I didn't have the power to resist.

He kept going off the script when we read through the first scene. It was him and me at the breakfast table, with David as the butler lurking in the background.

'Oh, Harris?' he summoned the butler and asked for his riding gear to be prepared, like it said in the script, and then he added a bit just for David: 'Oh and clean up this mess would you, there's a good lad.' He grinned, waving in the direction of the empty desk covered with make-believe breakfast things.

'Certainly sir, and could I get you anything else? A smack in the mouth perhaps?' David delivered his subtly-amended line completely deadpan, with a perfect butler bow, and Gemma and I both laughed.

You could tell David had that sneaky, wicked sense of humour that you could totally miss if you didn't pay attention. It was opposite to Anton's obvious, cheesy humour. They knew each other already, from a drama group, I think, and it seemed like they had their little dynamic worked out. They were like a comedy act, the way Anton delivered every look-at-me line with a grin and a wink and then, whenever he got out of hand, David cut him down with some clever, dry comment. You could tell they were good mates though, they were just doing that guy thing of showing affection through relentless assault.

We managed to read through most of the play despite dissolving into giggles quite a lot. I think we went a bit too far at times, because Steve's eyes would go a bit squinty and he screwed his mouth up disapprovingly into this hilarious cross, pointy little pout while he told us off, which didn't exactly make it easier to stop laughing.

The four of us went for a drink together afterwards and we laughed until we ached, mimicking Steve's funny expressions. Anton flirted some more while David's jokes stopped it all being too cheesy and cringey. David was shorter than Anton, and skinnier, and his blond hair was long enough that he had to keep sweeping it out of his eyes all the time. He had a kind of soft, gentle face. He told me he played keyboard in a band and I said I didn't know how he could fit it all in, as well as the play – and that he should let us know when he had a gig next.

We all talked about the old-fashionedness of the play and how it still felt real, even though it was from so long ago.

After just that day together, I couldn't imagine not having met them all. Thinking back to when I'd left the house that morning, it seemed like forever ago. I was on a high as I walked home, looking back on the day and feeling really part of something.

We packed four more rehearsals in before term started again in June. Steve was in a proper panic right from the start, going on about how we only had two months – about twenty rehearsals – to get everything perfect. Given each rehearsal was two or three hours long, and our play was quite short and just one of a bigger production, that sounded OK to me – but he was totally giving himself grey hairs about the fact we weren't going to be able to get into the theatre until really close to performance (he was livid that building works were running behind schedule but that the theatre managers insisted there was no need to move the performance dates back). He said we absolutely had to know our parts inside out before then so we could concentrate on sorting out the stage direction once we got in there.

After our first few sessions, he bought us all little *Foul Play* diaries (which was sweet, but also a shameless way to guilt us into making sure we didn't miss any rehearsals) and we put in one three-hour rehearsal every weekend, and a two-hour session one evening each week. But he wanted to increase that once the holidays started, and that was now not very far off at all.

We moaned about it later at our favourite hang-out near the college, a cool diner that did the best milkshakes and fries, and was open late. We'd already formed a habit of going there after rehearsals to chat, or run lines – or moan about what a slave-driver Steve was.

'My bandmates will be *well* displeased,' David said forlornly, looking at his diary.

'Tell me about it,' agreed Gemma. 'There's no way I'll get a proper summer job now all our weekends are all booked up. I'll be totally skint.'

'Don't worry about it,' Anton said. 'Come and work at the bowling alley with me. My uncle's the manager so I can get you a sweet deal on some easy shifts.' It was so typical Anton, he always had an answer. 'You too if you want, blondie,' he said, winking at me.

'That's Zoë or *Ms Nelson* to you, loser.' I fake-grinned at him, knowing I could probably make enough cash from my child-minding to tide me over. I loved that I didn't have to feel guilty about throwing insults at Anton. I knew his ego could take it. Plus he knew that I knew he was basically a good guy despite all the swagger.

'Always with the attitude, *Ms Nelson*.' He rolled his eyes at me and made a face that made me laugh.

Sometimes between rehearsals, it got so I craved seeing him, which worried me a bit. I wondered if I was getting a bit of a crush. But when I thought about it calmly, it was all three of them I loved being with, I was sure of it. Somehow,

24

as a group, we just worked. Gemma's excitable energy and Anton's flirting and boasting kept us all going, while David and I took turns being the voice of reason and teasing Anton. We just had such a laugh together.

I love Katy and Katie, don't get me wrong. Katy-with-a-*y* and all her dramas. She always has some guy dilemma or family feud going on and she loves to give you all the gory details – but she's super-clever and naughtily funny, so she could talk endlessly about anything and still be entertaining. Katie-with-an-*ie* is basically just the sweetest person you could meet. Always seeing the other person's point of view and looking for the best in everyone. They're such an odd couple that somehow they're closer for it, like they make up each other's missing bit to make a whole. School would've been horrible without them. We could always rely on each other if we needed to moan about school or stress at each other over coursework and stuff. But sometimes I felt like an outsider because their families were close – they even went on holiday together. Maybe it was my fault. They never treated me like a third thumb, or whatever that expression is, but they did have little in-jokes sometimes. Plus there was always a bit of me that worried I couldn't quite be me, because they knew me from school, where I was the quiet girl who kept her head down.

I couldn't remember ever having a proper, physically exhausting laugh with them like I had with Gemma, Anton and David. That was the great thing about being able to meet people outside school. It was a chance to start fresh. Plus it was just nice to hang out with blokes, because at school it was all girls, hence all the bitchy crowds.

I don't know why I let my life at school bother me. It's not like I cared what any of them thought of me – neither did the Katies because they weren't part of a big gang either. But a lot of people seemed to think I was stuck-up or something, because I wasn't loud and giggly like a lot of other girls, or obsessed with hair and make-up and fashion. (I'm not saying I don't like make-up and fashion, by the way, just that I might have different ideas of what I like. Anyway, I know there's more important things in life than hair extensions and fake nails.) I tell myself over and over that I don't care what they think of me, and most of the time I'm convinced, but I admit maybe I'm a little tiny bit scared too, and that means I don't give anyone a chance. I'm not a psychologist or a psychotherapist or anything, so I don't know, but maybe I close myself off a bit, for protection. What if I did try to make friends, and they *did* see the real me, and they still didn't like me? More rejection.

Anyway, whatever odd things go on in this head of mine, it was the best feeling, finally thinking maybe I wasn't so weird after all – I could have a real group of great mates and just have a laugh like anyone else.

That summer, in between rehearsing, going to David's gigs and getting sneaky discounted games at the bowling alley, the four of us would spend all the time we could hanging out in the diner or in the park by the college.

We were together all the time and I can't remember ever being happier. Back then, I couldn't have imagined that anything could change how close we were.

Chapter 4

It was close to the end of term in July when Steve finally told us the theatre was ready. He said we'd been doing so well that, if we wanted to, we could pop along on Saturday and just have a look round instead of having a full rehearsal, before we got in there for real on the Wednesday to 'get to work' as he put it. We all agreed we'd like to. I think we were excited to get up on a stage – we'd got to the point where we all knew our lines and we were sick of just using a classroom with all the tables and chairs pushed up against the walls.

Just when everything was going so well though, on the Friday night before our theatre visit, I got a call from Gemma. When I saw her name come up on my phone, I got a weird, nervous knot in my stomach. She asked if we could meet at the diner, just the two of us, before we met the boys at the station. As I agreed to go, I wasn't sure whether to be worried or not. The diner was close to the college but was the other end of town from the theatre really (and an extra walk for me as I lived at the theatre end). It made me wonder if she had something nasty to tell me and wanted to be in familiar, happy surroundings. Why couldn't she say whatever it was over the phone?

When I walked in, she was already sitting down with a Coke and was jiggling nervously, just like that first day we'd met.

'You worried about something?' I asked her as I sat down. I was half joking, but she confirmed my instincts were right.

'Argh, am I so easy to work out?' She rolled her eyes. 'Well, I wanted to ask you something. And I guess I'm a bit unsure how to put it.'

Oh man, that sounded serious. I wasn't sure I wanted to hear it.

'Mmhmm.' I tried to seem nonchalant.

'Anton asked me out. And I wanted to check with you before I said yes for sure. I reeeeally like him, Zoë, but I sort of got the impression maybe you do too, and I wanted to check with you it wouldn't be weird if I said yes.' She peered at me as if she wanted to try to work out my reaction from my face. 'We've all been getting on so well, I don't want it to go bad. I don't want you to think I went behind your back or anything.'

It was a lot to take in and I wasn't sure how I felt.

Mostly, I felt relieved – was that all she'd wanted to ask? But then maybe I did fancy Anton a little bit, now that she said it, and I did feel a weird little pang of jealousy. But what was the point in admitting it when he'd chosen her?

'That's great, Gemma,' I said with a grin.

She raised her eyebrows at me, still peering at my face – I saw then why she'd insisted on having the conversation in person.

'Say yes! Honestly, it wouldn't be weird. Of course say yes, I can't believe you asked my permission – you're so funny.' Of course, what I really meant was that it was sweet of her and that I appreciated it.

'Are you sure? I know you'd say it was fine even if it wasn't, for my sake, because you're a nice person, but are you *sure* you don't like him too? I really do want to know, or I wouldn't ask . . .'

Oh, why did she have to go and flipping ask me outright? I knew I wouldn't be able to just say no and leave it at that. It's like I've got some sort of naturally-occurring truth serum in my blood or something. Ask me a question, and I just spill my guts out . . .

'No, no,' I said. Stop there, Zoë, I told myself. But I didn't listen. 'I don't think so, not properly – I mean you can't help getting sucked in by his cheeky grin, can you?'

She nodded. Her face lit up when she thought of him and in that moment I suddenly knew that I felt really, truly happy for her.

'No, honestly, Gemma, that flirty banter we have? That's not sexual tension, you know, he just genuinely gets on my nerves!'

She laughed loudly and seemed to relax.

'I know what you mean about how great things have been and not wanting to risk it, but I don't see why this should have to change anything. Just don't try and pair me off with David now, OK? I don't want this play turning into some icky, loved-up double date.'

'Aw, thanks Zoë.' Gemma grinned at me and grabbed my hand across the table. 'I promise we won't leave you alone with David – not the whole time anyway!'

I was impressed at how grown-up the whole conversation was – and how easy. As we finished our drinks and went to meet the others, I felt all warm and fuzzy. It was like we'd crossed a friendship milestone somehow, because we'd faced a potential problem and got past it. When we spotted the guys, David came over to walk beside me and Anton gravitated towards Gemma. She reached for his hand and I watched him smile at her – a real, genuine, lovely smile just for her, not a cheesy grin – and I felt this huge surge of emotion for them.

Don't get me wrong, as a human being (a boyfriendless, female human being), I'm not saying I didn't feel a tiny twinge of jealousy, but it wasn't because I wanted to be with Anton; it was because I wanted someone of my own to smile a smile like that, just for me.

I got over it though. And, as we all trooped to the theatre together, it was like we were a team. Ready for anything.

Even though the theatre wasn't far at all from the centre of town, I'd never really stopped to look at it. It was set back from the road, behind a canopy of trees, a car park and one of those flimsy, boxy community buildings. Even when you got to it, it was shrouded in yet more trees, which obscured it from view despite the leaves being parched by the summer weather already. It wasn't until you were quite close that you got the full sense of the building. I stopped for a moment as we got our first proper view of it, and my stomach did a little flip as if I'd found out a secret I wasn't sure I wanted to know.

It felt imposing, because it sort of snuck up on you and was looming over you before you even really knew it was there. But there was something slightly comical about the grand features of it, given its size. For a smallish, tucked-away building, its little dome entrance, pillars and steps that spilled down to the ground seemed a bit boastful. And I don't know as much as I'd like about architecture, but it seemed an odd mix of sort of Roman-ish pillars and then tall, thin patterned strips of window that reminded me of some of Dad's books on art deco.

Most of all, though, it seemed like it was alive. You know the way you look at your toys when you're little and you're so sure they all come to life the moment your back's turned? It was like that, only I didn't want to turn my back. For a moment I was captured, frozen, trying and failing to imagine its past. Then Gemma called back over her shoulder to hurry me up and I came round.

There were loads of people rushing about as we walked into the grand foyer. They were all dressed in black and I guessed they were all new theatre staff – security and technical people. Some of them were moving boxes or ladders or paint tins around and a couple of them had Bluetooth headsets on and were striding about talking to invisible others, looking important. It was like MI5 had invaded, only a bit scruffier.

Steve was talking to one of the 'men in black' (only she was a woman) and beckoned us over for our little tour. We looked around the front of the theatre – the café and box office and an arched doorway with a sign over it saying *History room*. It was going to be like a tiny museum of all the old stuff they found while they were renovating that was too interesting to chuck out. Then there was the auditorium. That was the best bit. It was dark and velvety and glamorous and, as we looked over the backs of all the seats, up to the stage, I knew we were all feeling the same excitement, knowing that in just a couple of weeks we'd be standing up there, looking down at a real audience. I imagined everyone in their seats, and all of us in our costumes . . . The others headed over to the stage and goose bumps prickled my skin. There was no going back now.

Chapter 5

'We've got hours and hours completely to ourselves . . .'
Anton said his line. That was my cue to come on stage and
catch him at it with 'the other woman'.

I stepped out from the deep shadows of the wings and
on to the stage. The others turned to look at me – Gemma,
Anton and, just visible in the wings on the other side,
David was watching patiently.

'Why . . . Rebecca, darling . . . I thought you'd left over
an hour ago. I . . .'

Then it was my line. We'd done it dozens of times
before but this was the first time on this stage. Was it
excitement, or a renewed bout of nerves that was making
me dizzy? Maybe it was the smell of the place that was
making me nauseous – a queasy mix of musty old, and
synthetic, freshly painted new.

My friends' faces were pointed at me expectantly, waiting for my words, but when I tried to speak, the words got stuck. The edges of my vision were starting to blur and darken. I tried to swallow the sticky, sick feeling in my throat, but I couldn't budge the muscles. Was this stage fright? Suddenly I was cut off from my body, I couldn't feel my arms or legs properly. I'd never felt anything like it before. I thought I was passing out. I expected to fall down any second and for everything to go black. But it didn't, everything was just blurry at the edges.

I could see what was in front of me but I was detached from it, like I'd somehow been sucked into a dream. I could hear Anton string out his line, trying to help me along, but his words were muffled, as if I was listening from another room.

Then I heard my line. Out it came, perfectly clearly. But I hadn't said anything – I mean, I was sure I hadn't moved my lips. I could barely even *feel* my lips.

What was happening?

It was like I was hypnotised. Maybe someone else had said the line, but I was sure there hadn't been anyone behind me . . . and the voice sounded like mine . . . I think.

It must have been mine, because in that second, the others unclenched. The awkward pause was over and the play sprang back into life. It all started to flow along again, without me. Only it wasn't without me. Not from what they could tell. I started moving around the stage, not quite

35

according to what we'd rehearsed, but near enough.

'I'm sorry to disappoint you, Tristan,' my voice continued. I was acting, just carrying on with the play, but I wasn't controlling my movements. It was terrifying. I'd have been crying out to my friends with fear, begging them to help me – except I couldn't. I was imprisoned. It was like when you're trying to scream in a nightmare, but no sound comes out because back in the real world your body's paralysed in sleep.

'Wh . . . don't be silly, darling,' Anton said, and, helplessly, I watched the rehearsal play out in front of me, anticipating my lines and hearing them come out but not having any hand in saying them. My tone and emphasis were different, but clearly not enough for people to be put off. I was willing them to notice, for Steve, the director, to call time out. I was desperate for them to see something was wrong. But they didn't. They all just went on as if everything was normal.

At the end of the scene, after Rebecca gets shot, they had to carry me off stage, which they did. And as they moved the set around for the next scene, in the cellar, my body just watched everything go on around it. No one even gave me a second look.

No one except this one guy, who was standing in the wings on the other side of the stage. He was dressed in black like the other staff, so I assumed he was a stagehand. He was looking right at me. He was young, only a little bit older than us I guessed, maybe nineteen. He was amazing-looking – sort of boyish and manly at once, with smooth, innocent features but strong shoulders and arms . . . His perfect jawline was lightly shadowed with a hint of stubble. He had dark, longish-short hair and these huge, blue, piercing eyes. I think my heart was racing faster as I watched him watch me. It was like he could see me in a way none of the others could. For a moment it was like he could see right into my soul.

Did he know what was happening to me? For a just second it seemed like it. But then Anton stepped between us and I lost sight of him.

Carrying me back on for the next scene, Gemma and Anton put me down centre stage, on the little couch, and covered me with a throw. I was a 'dead' body while they acted over me. I wondered if the stagehand was still there, just a metre or two away, watching. My body stayed frustratingly still, obedient to stage directions but not to me. If I'd had control of it, I would have peeked to see if he was there. I was sure he could see that something terrifying was happening to me.

'OK guys, stop there!' Steve clapped his hands loudly. 'That was pretty good, well done.' My head lifted itself, throwing off the shroud, and turned to face him as he was rising from his seat. 'It's all sounding nice, but I think we're going to need to adjust some of the directions a bit – they're a bit lost in the change of scale. I think all of your gestures and your volume will need to come up a notch, too.' He wafted his arm up like he was conducting an orchestra. 'We're not in a cosy classroom any more. Why don't you take five, get a drink, limber up and try and "think big" so we can read the next scene with a bit more oomph, hmm?' With a grin and another suitably theatrical wave of his hand to signal break time, Steve turned back to his chair and his notes. Gemma's voice was suddenly behind me.

'Come on, Zoë, let's check out that café thing in the foyer – I need a juice or something.' I watched her loom in front of me, sit at the front of the stage, swing her legs over the edge and jump down. My mind wanted to follow but my body didn't move.

She spun round. 'Coming? You OK?' she quizzed me with a slight frown. I nodded, I think, and then went downstage right, behind the curtain, down some steps and out of the door at the side of the stage, where Gemma was waiting with her hands on her hips.

'You're acting weird. Come on, let's get snacks.'

I followed as she walked to the back of the auditorium and out into the foyer. How strange to be moving around without the sensation of walking – it was like I was a toddler again, being carried wherever I had to go, with no choice. The boys were heading out of the front of the building, Anton had a pack of cigarettes in his hand as he waved at us. Gemma waved back.

'I wish he'd pack that in.'

'What?' I heard my voice ask, even though I didn't want to say it. I didn't understand how it was happening.

'Waving. I just hate it,' Gemma joked. 'I mean smoking, obviously.'

'Why? Everyone smokes. It's good for your nerves . . .' What was I talking about?

'What are you talking about, Zoë? You don't. I don't . . . Not often anyway.' She gave me a quick sheepish look, but my face obviously didn't register it, because her expression quickly went blank again.

'"Smoking Kills"'?' Gemma tried again, peering at me and waggling inverted-comma fingers. 'Besides, it makes his breath stink when I get up close.' She winked at me. I wanted to climb out of my head. I wanted my body back so I could smile at her. I had no idea what my face was doing.

In the café, my hypnotised brain seemed to be transfixed by the rows of sandwiches and drinks in the chill cabinet. I could hear Gemma was still talking to me but I couldn't turn to look at her. Inside I was shouting at myself to wake up.

'You were doing your lines differently today,' she said.

'Better?' my voice replied. Nice and modest.

'I don't know, I liked the way you did it before as well, you know, sort of gentler, with a bit of vulnerability.'

'Vulnerable is just another way of saying weak. No one's going to feel sorry for me when you steal my husband, if I'm all weak. They'll just think I brought it on myself.'

Where was *this* coming from? It couldn't be from inside my head.

'You mean when *Diana* steals *Rebecca's* husband? I don't know if the audience is supposed to feel sorry for Rebecca or not. I'm not sure it's that simple . . .'

'Oh, it's the simplest, oldest story there is. The typical man plays away with the younger, tackier, obvious, tart-type. Of course the audience is supposed to side with me.' Wait. What was I saying? I didn't mean that! Shut up!

'You mean side with *Rebecca*.' I could hear the edge creeping into Gemma's voice. She was getting annoyed and I didn't blame her.

'Do I?' my voice challenged. Oh. My. GOD. Shut up, shut up! The edge in my voice matched hers and raised her a notch. Why? I didn't want to fight with her. There was no way this stuff was coming from my brain, even under hypnosis or if I was ill or something. Someone must have drugged me somehow. Suddenly I wondered if I was dying.

I was filled with panic but there was nothing I could do. I could see Gemma now, my face was pointed right at her and I didn't know what expression I had on, but I could see hers all too clearly. And her hands were on her hips.

'Well, it seems to me like, if you *don't*, that's a sly way of calling *me* a "tacky tart" or whatever granny phrase you just used. So what *do* you mean?'

'Excuse me. I think I'm going to go outside for some air.' Good! Get out before you lose a friend.

The foyer opened up in front of me as I turned and left the café. The new glass in the windows was still covered so it was dark, despite the bright sunshine outside. My eyes gradually acclimatised, making out the patterns on the old-fashioned but newly polished, marble-type floor. It looked cool to the touch. There was a great circle with huge, elongated, arrow-like stripes, like on Dad's old backgammon board – only they emanated out in a ring from the centre. My eyes moved up to look into the domed ceiling. More and more, the building itself seemed to want to whisper secrets in my ear, but all I could hear for real was the miles-away-seeming shouts and traffic from outside on the street.

A slice of glinting sunlight was reaching in through the doors and my body gradually moved towards it. I moved through the doors, into the blinding brightness and on to the broad, shallow steps that spilled on to the pavement. Then I was rushing, zooming back into life. My senses rushed back into me, stinging like the sudden pain of saliva surging into your mouth on a first bite.

I think I fainted then, because the next thing I remember is seeing the fleshy red of sunlight through my eyelids. I could hear Anton's voice. Then, in the shadow of David's head looming over me, I opened my eyes using my will and my muscles, which – thank you, thank God – were connected again. I couldn't help laughing, and there was the sound coming out, the sound of me making myself laugh. I could hear everything back in the real world like I'd burst back up to the surface from underwater. I asked my arms to reach up and they did what they were told. I held on to Anton's forearm with my left hand and David's with my right and they helped me up. I was shaking and I wanted to cry with relief and shock.

'Are you all right? What happened?' asked David.

'Mmhmm,' was all I could say. I gave a wobbly nod.

'That was some nice passing out there, Zoë. You smacked right down on the floor. You're lucky you didn't split your head open.' Anton sounded almost impressed.

'You hurt anywhere?' David sat me back down on the steps and sent Anton for some water. My knee did hurt, and my arm. I could see some skin had come off by my elbow and there were a few little blood speckles. But I was OK. It was all over, I was OK, it had just been some kind of weird fainting fit.

Anton reappeared with water and Gemma was following behind. She looked worried but stood back a little and let the boys fuss over me.

'I'm sorry,' I said, looking at Gemma first, then the others. 'But I'm feeling properly weird. I think I'm gonna have to go home. Will you say sorry to Steve for me, too, for flaking out on rehearsal?'

'Sure, sure.' David went to help me up. 'I think we should put her in a cab though, guys, in case she passes out again. How much cash have you got?'

The guys were so sweet. They called me a taxi, gave me a few extra quid for the fare and told me to text when I got home so they knew I was safe. When I got in I sent them a thank you message. Then my head started to crowd with thoughts of what had happened. It wasn't normal, I was sure of it. I thought of the guy in the wings at the theatre. I could see his face as clearly as if he was standing in front of me. I felt an odd sort of rush thinking of the way he looked at me, his expression was charged with something but, as precisely as I could remember the look in his eyes, I couldn't read it. The more I argued with myself that I'd just had a dizzy spell, that people just faint sometimes – especially in the middle of a summer day, the more I thought of his face. He flooded my head – not just because he was amazingly, stunningly attractive, but because he'd been the one person there who seemed to know something was happening to me, while it was happening.

But it was over and I didn't want to think too much. I was so tired. I got into bed and tried to make my mind blank, sinking into the soft safety of my pillow. I kept remembering those dark edges that had crept into my eyes and, although it wasn't cold, I shivered and drew my duvet in closer. The last thing that went through my mind as I drifted into sleep was the stagehand's wonderful face and that strange look.

Chapter 6

At a silly hour in the morning, I woke up aching. It was just before six a.m. and I thought I must be really ill. I'd expected to sleep for an hour or so and instead I'd passed out for about twelve. I'd never fainted before. If I was ill, at least that would explain it. What else could explain that horrible experience? All the thoughts I'd managed to fight off the evening before came rushing back, mixing with odd feelings left over from my sleep.

I'd had really vivid, weird dreams like I often have if I'm running a temperature. I lay there, trying to remember as much as I could of what had played out in my mind during the night. I chased after the quickly fragmenting, disappearing images, like I was trying to make out the shape of an impression left in a cushion before it could spring back flat.

I'd been back in the theatre, only it had looked different, sort of tatty and lurid. I was backstage I think, but I didn't recognise much as I rushed from room to room to room. I was angry about something – really furious, the rage had been bursting through me – and each room I went into, I'd throw things on to the floor and smash things against the walls. I was opening drawers and emptying everything out, but I didn't know what I was looking for. I had an odd sense of time running out, like I was being chased, but I hadn't seen any other people in the building, it had felt quite dark and deserted. I seemed to be going through all these different doors of all different sizes, like something from *Alice in Wonderland*, and I'd fought through swathes of curtain and come out on to the stage.

I was standing on that spot on the stage where I'd had my fit or whatever it was the day before. And there was the stagehand, watching me with that same mysterious look in his eyes; he was trying to come towards me, but something seemed to be stopping him and he seemed to be struggling. Then, something knocked the breath out of me and I looked up into the space above the stage where the rigging and lights are. I just stared, until I started floating upwards through the maze of metal and wires and out through the top of the theatre into the sky, as if there were no roof. It was night and, as I floated higher and higher, in patches of yellowy light below, I could see the tops of houses and trees. I'd had flying dreams before, but usually, I'd be moving quite fast and feeling quite euphoric. This time I'd been just sort of drifting and I didn't feel good at all, quite desperate actually.

I wanted to write everything down before I forgot, but as I sat myself up to get a pen and notebook out of my bedside table, pain shot through my hands and made me wince. I pulled them out from under the duvet and was freaked out to see scratches and cuts all over them. What had I been doing in my sleep? I wasn't a sleepwalker normally, more like the opposite – it often took me a few minutes after waking up to be able to move. I got up and checked myself over in the mirror. I had sore patches on my legs too, and the grazes from falling over on the steps. I wondered if bruises might start to appear over the next few days. Apart from all that, and the messed-up hands, I seemed OK. I looked at myself in the mirror for a while. It was the same old me. The same old bed hair, that slightly ginger blond that wasn't properly pretty blond or a nice fiery red but somewhere rubbish in between. The same old messy freckles.

I let the sensible voice in my head convince me everything was fine and normal and what happened the day before was just a one-off and finished with. I was a bit ill with something. It would pass.

I'd left a note for Dad when I got in the day before to say I wasn't feeling good and he'd obviously let me sleep right through till morning. He'd be getting up in an hour or so and I wondered whether to tell him about fainting. I decided not to this time. If it happened again, I'd tell him; but I knew he'd just get worried and, if it was a one-off, there was no point in putting him through it. He'd probably insist on taking me to the doctor and I knew all he wanted to do was concentrate on the book he was trying to write – he was spending as much time as he could in the library at work, or the study at home. He had enough on his plate without worrying about me.

When he knocked softly on my door at about seven-thirty, I was sitting up in bed, trying to read.

'Come in,' I called.

'I'm off to the library in a minute,' he said. 'How are you feeling?'

'Oh, I'm OK, just a bit icky, think I might be getting a cold or something,' I lied. I figured I'd just act headachy and lie low for the day, pursuing my traditional holiday pastimes: napping, reading, eating and watching TV.

'Can I get you anything? Do you want me to stay?'

'No, I'm OK thanks,' I smiled. 'There's soup and juice and everything I need downstairs. I'll sort myself out. You go.'

He nodded and smiled back at me. 'Feel better, sweetpea.'

Hopefully a day of rest would see off the strange lurgy and I could still go to the rehearsal the next day. I worried how Gemma would act with me and I thought about telling her what had happened. But when I imagined trying to explain it, I couldn't think what I'd say that didn't sound ridiculous, or like I was making excuses.

I kept trying to read but none of the words were going in. Everything was going round and round in my head. The things I'd said to Gemma, and where on earth they'd come from. That sick feeling, the terror of losing my senses. The stagehand – those piercing eyes.

Watching TV was a better distraction, but there was only so much daytime rubbish I could watch before my mind started wandering again. So I called Katie.

'If you're feeling up to it, come over.' She made the offer I'd hoped she would when I said I was ill but bored. 'Katy's coming over in a bit, too. We were going to talk holiday plans, but we'll try not to be too boring if you want to join us? It'll be good to see you – we're flying out first thing on Friday, so we've only got a couple of days . . .'

'That'd be nice, thanks. I'll get changed and come over now if that's OK?'

'Yay – sure thing, see you in a bit.'

I could see that Katy had already arrived when I walked down Katie's drive; she was perched on a stool at the breakfast bar, with her back to me, waving her arms wildly. She'd obviously launched straight into a story. I quickened my pace, not wanting to miss out.

'We're just discussing "*the dinner with Justyn*",' Katie tipped me off as she opened the door. I clapped my hands together. There had been much build-up to the dinner:

Katy-with-a-*y* finally goes out with Justyn-with-a-*y*. We rushed through to the kitchen, knowing Katy could only be put on hold for seconds before she'd overheat. I smiled to myself, imagining smoke coming out of her, her vocal brake pads struggling against the outpouring of her urgent news.

'I swear to you, honestly – hi Zoë – I might as well have been one of those blow-up dolls.'

'Er, what?' I looked bemusedly over at Katie, wondering what exactly I'd missed, and nodded as she brandished teabags in silent offer.

'For all the attention he paid me,' Katy continued, 'after all the *hassle* he gave me to get me to go out with him. You remember – he'd wait at the school gates in the morning . . . and then he started with all the creepy Bluetoothing – all that agonising I went through: was it too weird and obsessive or should I cut him a break . . .' Katie put my mug down in front of me and I smiled thanks. 'Well, I've concluded I made a big mistake because I *finally* say yes to him, and then we're sitting there, and he's looking over my shoulder the whole night – it was like I could have been anybody. And I'm sure he was looking at the other girls in the restaurant, too. What is all *that* about?'

'Maybe he was nervous?' Katie offered. 'It doesn't necessarily mean he wasn't glad you were there.'

But Katy wasn't having any platitudes. 'Well, he had his chance. I'm not going through that again, he can go for

49

pizza on his own next time to ogle. I really don't know what was going through his mind – Zoë, what have you been doing? What's with the state of your hands?' Katy sneaked the question in, totally underhand, mid-sentence, and with that, allowed herself to pause for a sip of tea. It took me a bit off guard when I was just enjoying having my mind taken off everything.

'Oh. I'm not sure, I think I was doing weird things in my sleep. I woke up and they were like that.' I said it over the top of my mug, thinking that might be enough for Katy and she'd go back into her story, but there was an unusual pause and they both looked at me, slightly puzzled. OK then, let's talk about it, I thought. It might actually be a relief. 'I had some weird dreams, after I fainted yesterday . . .'

'You fainted? Are you OK? What happened?' Katie looked worried. It actually felt good to say it out loud, so I carried on.

'Actually, it was the weirdest thing, I'm a bit freaked out by it. I'm not sure what happened but I felt sick – we were on stage – and everything went dark, but I didn't faint until later, like maybe about half an hour, forty-five minutes later, when I left the building.' I looked into my tea as I remembered. 'The weird bit is, I was walking and talking but without controlling it myself. My lines were coming out but I wasn't saying them. And then when we had a break, I was talking to Gemma, you know, the other girl in the play, and it was like I wasn't me. I was saying stuff but I honestly didn't know where the words were coming from. It was almost like I was *hypnotised*, or . . .' I happened to glance up then, and the Katies' faces stopped me in my tracks. I caught a glimpse of them looking at each other oddly and it dawned on me how I must sound. They looked back at me and tried to look concerned, but even Katie had an odd hint of something I didn't like, like she was thinking I was losing it. I backtracked as best I could.

'Anyway, I passed out on the steps outside, just for a few seconds, and got a few grazes.'

'And the dreams?' Katy pushed me, but there was a look in her eye that made me think I ought to tread carefully so as not to sound insane.

'Oh, I just dreamed about the theatre; it's this spooky building, and there was this lovely stagehand guy who was watching me, us . . .' The image of him filled my head again and I couldn't help blushing.

'*Stagehand guy?*' Katy jumped in.

I was so busy thinking about him, I didn't stop to worry about how I sounded, I just blurted, 'Oh my *goodness*. He was the most beautiful guy I've seen in – well, forever.'

Katy let out a high pitched 'Ahhaaaa!' and clapped her hands together excitedly. 'Now we're getting to the bottom of this dizzy spell!' she exclaimed at top volume.

Katie giggled. 'You *never* fancy anyone, Zoë – that's great.'

I'd only dated once since we all started secondary school

51

together. But we didn't talk about Joe – not after he dumped me to get back together with his ex. They were forever nagging me about boys though, because I never did fancy anyone. Until now.

'Details please,' Katy demanded.

'Oh *no*,' I said, kicking myself for my loose tongue but grateful the subject change had stopped them looking at me like I was nuts. 'I didn't even speak to him, let's not get ahead of ourselves.' When I thought about going back to the theatre, I got a rush of excitement that he might be there, mixed with the dread of going back after yesterday's drama. 'I've got another rehearsal on Wednesday,' I said sheepishly. 'Maybe he'll be there. I'll keep you posted.'

'You'd better,' Katy warned. 'Ugh, he has to be better than *Justyn* – I can't believe he even let me *pay half* after that. I only offered thinking he'd refuse . . .' And that was the end of my share of the attention, thank goodness.

It was great to switch off for the rest of the afternoon and let the Katies tell me about their holiday plans and help with wardrobe/packing decisions. As I walked home though, I thought of how they'd reacted when I'd tried to explain what had happened. I realised that if even my closest friends weren't ready to hear about this then I was on my own.

Maybe there wasn't anything to worry about, it was over after all. I berated myself for over-thinking it and told myself it must have just been straightforward lightheadedness – the heat, dehydration, not eating enough. But every time I tried to convince myself it was nothing, I thought of him. And the look on his face, which was seared in my brain, sent me back to thinking there was more to all this than a plain old dizzy spell.

Chapter 7

'Had any more girly fainting fits since we saw you last?' said Anton when I found the others at a table in the theatre café just before rehearsal. I guess that was his idea of asking how I was. I shook my head.

We sat and chatted for a while and it was good to feel a bit more normal about being back. As soon as I got a minute alone with Gemma, though, I said I was sorry for before and that I didn't know why I'd said what I said unless it was because I was ill. She gave me a thin smile.

'Don't worry about it. You feeling better?' She touched my arm and seemed honest about asking. I was relieved she seemed to have just about forgiven me.

'I think so,' I said as we walked through to the auditorium.

'OK folks, seeing as we've got most of our costumes

54

and props sorted now, let's have a quick walk through for direction, as a reminder and so we can catch Zoë up on what she missed last time, and then we'll try and do the whole play right through.' Steve pushed his hands together like he was praying and made one of his pursed-lips faces. 'I'm going to try my *best* not to interrupt because we're getting to the point now where we need to get used to doing full run-throughs. OK? Just try to remember all the things we've been working on and give it your best, yes?' He was all hyper and excited – and it was infectious.

We dumped our stuff backstage and, secretly, I looked around, searching for a glimpse of the stagehand. But there was no sign of him and I was surprised by how deflated I felt.

As we did a super-fast walk through, I made notes on my script so I could revise the stage direction changes later. Then Steve made us each sit where the audience would be while he stood in for us, one by one, so we could see how much bigger our gestures needed to be. He was right. What we thought was totally OTT on stage actually looked and sounded about right if you were the one watching.

We took ten minutes' break and all chatted outside. It was a grey day but heavy with heat. One of those days when you wish for a thunderstorm to clear the air. A couple of staff walked past us in their black shirts and I felt a flash of anger at myself when I thought of the stagehand again. This was getting obsessive. I needed to get over it. I tried to focus on Anton's story about some crazy guy they'd had to throw out of the bowling alley.

Back on stage, the first scene at the breakfast table went without a single mistake – it was perfect. Then I got to relax for a bit because the second act was mostly Gemma and Anton. I was having a great time watching them be brilliant – and peeking at Steve, who was doing a surprisingly good job of keeping quiet but was furiously writing notes.

Then came the third act, the bit where Rebecca walks in on her husband and Diana together in their house. I was so caught up watching the first bit of the scene I was hardly thinking about the last rehearsal – it all seemed so long ago.

'We've got hours and hours completely to ourselves . . .' said Anton. I stepped out on to the stage and did my best 'stiff-British-upper-lip repressed shock and rage' expression. 'Why . . . Rebecca, darling . . . I thought you'd left over an hour ago. I . . .'

I felt dizzy.

No, no, no! It was happening again. I could feel the gust of nausea coming. I reached up to clutch my head and tried to say, 'No, stop!' but it came out as a whisper. All in a second I knew panicking was useless. I looked at everyone's faces and wanted to cry – but I couldn't know if my face showed any fear. I didn't have time to let them know what was going on.

I saw David's expectant expression, willing me on from the wings. There, behind him, someone emerged out of the shadows. It was him. The stagehand. He was looking right at me again. This time, though, his face flashed with shock and concern. He seemed to take a step towards me. I felt a rush of hope. Could he help?

In that moment, he was the most beautiful thing I'd ever seen. Just like last time, it was like he was the only one who knew something was wrong with me. His expression had such kindness in it, even though there was fear there too. What could he see that no one else could? To everyone else, I was just me. To him, I looked wrong, for whatever reason; it was obvious he knew something I didn't.

I tried to reach out to him but I'd already lost control. As that horribly familiar feeling of paralysis started to take hold of me, every part of my instinct and will wanted to move towards him, this person whose name I didn't even know but who was suddenly everything to me. But I was frozen, locked again inside a body that was being stolen from me. I saw him hesitate and back off, retreating behind David into the darkness.

Don't leave me! I wanted to scream. Maybe it was because I'd dreamed about him, but it felt like we were connected, tied together by flesh and blood and nerves somehow, because as I watched him disappear into the dark it hurt, like part of me was tearing.

There was absolutely nothing I could do then, except wait. Wait and hope I'd get my body back again. Just when I felt like I'd clawed my way back to reality from last time, made my excuses and smoothed over the damage, it was all happening again.

'So it seems.' I heard my voice reply and just like before, the play came back to life. 'I'm sorry to disappoint you, Tristan.'

'Wh . . . don't be silly, darling, it's a lovely surprise. Di . . . er, Miss Baker here was just measuring me up for a suit. I thought I'd give Stokes and Sons a call and order something new for the Robinsons' bash. What do you think?' Anton delivered the perfect lying cad speech.

'What do I think? I think *you* must think I'm an utter *fool*, trying to sell me that line. I also think I can tell the difference between a bespoke tailor and an adulterous hussy perfectly well, thank you.' It was my voice again but that wasn't quite what I was supposed to say.

'Hold on, Zoë,' called Steve, breaking his silence. 'The line is just, "I can tell the difference between bespoke tailoring and adultery, thank you." Remember? Carry on though.'

'Oh, I'm sorry.' The voice coming out didn't sound like me, but it was. I admit I can be sarcastic sometimes but this was way beyond that, my tone was positively vicious. I just didn't talk like that – it was creepy. 'I must have misremembered – "hussy" just felt so appropriate.' My face turned towards Gemma.

'Well, I think it's a bit much,' Steve warned me. 'It tips over from funny to malicious. And this is supposed to be a comedy, remember? Dark, yes, but not heavy. I'm always open to ideas but let's stick to the script on this one, shall we?'

My eyes were still pointed right at Gemma and she was staring directly back at me. I could see hurt and anger in her face. She's a sweet person but she can stand up for herself too. I loved that about her. I knew she wouldn't take much more of this. I was on thin ice and it was cracking right in front of me. What could I do? I was powerless to stop it. Anton came to the rescue with his line.

'Listen, Rebecca darling, you've got it all wrong, the truth is —'

'The truth is finally out. That's what the truth is. And I want *you* out too. Tonight. I'll give you an hour to pack some things. *Your* things, that is. Do be careful not to take anything of mine, won't you, Tristan, or it might be more than adultery you're accused of when I get my lawyer on to this.' My line came out OK this time and I turned to walk away, like I was supposed to, so that Tristan, horrified at the thought of losing his nice life of luxury, could make a grab for the gun in the sideboard and shoot me, or rather Rebecca, in a moment of madness. That was when the other two went into a panic and decided to lock me in the cellar.

My hijacked head, it seemed, had other ideas though. Before Anton could get his line out and shoot me in the back, I swung round, lunged at him and punched him full in the stomach.

I've never punched anyone in my life. I could feel the force of it jolt my arm despite my dulled senses and it hurt. Not only did I have to watch helplessly as I punched my friend completely against my will, I also had to feel the physical pain of it. Things happened so quickly then. I think Steve jumped up but he can't have been quick enough . . .

'What the hell are you *doing*?' screamed Gemma. It was a good question. I wouldn't have had an answer even if I'd been able to speak for myself. I was in a living, breathing nightmare where my will and reason was folded away somewhere unreachable. She rushed forward to help Anton, who was doubled over. I think I might have even winded him because he was breathing awkwardly. But as soon as she touched him I went for her. I could feel this anger inside me and I just didn't understand where it was coming from.

'Take your hands off him, you WITCH,' my voice spat as I launched towards her and grabbed her arms hard, prising them away from Anton. I felt my fingernails dig in. She cried out and pulled away.

'What the —' Before she could get a sentence out I slapped her hard in the face.

Steve grabbed me then, taking hold of my arms from behind. I stamped on his feet and he yelped but kept hold of me, thank goodness. My body was fighting against him but I was willing him to win. I wanted him to just pick me up and hurl me out of the theatre – once I got outside I'd be back. I could be me again.

He dragged me away, through the auditorium and into the foyer, where he gave me a talking to.

'You need to go home and cool off, young lady,' he fumed. My expression must have been defiant, or blank – because he carried on. 'It's too late now to get someone else for your part, but I promise you this: no matter about all the work we've all put into this, I will cancel the whole play if I have to. If you can't do some damned *growing up . . .*' I was just willing him to stop talking and force me out of the door – all I wanted was to get out.

He folded his arms and marched me towards the exit. The sky outside was still thunderous but ought to be turning dusky soon and cooler. I couldn't wait to feel the air on my skin and the rush of all my senses coming back.

But, as I watched my feet move over the threshold of marble to stone and tentatively take the steps down to the pavement, I felt nothing. I was still submerged in this dark pool. There was no rushing up to the surface, no release.

Why? Why wasn't my nightmare ending – this was where it had ended last time. What did it mean?

Was that it? Was I gone forever, trapped? My panic was cut off from my senses, the racing heart and shaky hands I should have had weren't there, but the feeling was real. Wishing and willing myself to come round just didn't work. I simply watched as my body walked past familiar houses, hedges, paths and turns, and took me home.

The hallway was getting dark when I came in through the back door. Dad popped his head out from his study. My eyes looked at him, but I said nothing.

'You're early,' he said. I was still silent as I hung my jacket up by the door. Dad took the rudeness as a sign I was upset.

'Are you OK, Zo? What's happened?'

'She stole him,' I hissed aggressively, spinning round to face him. All I wanted to do was say hi, smile, offer a cup of tea . . . Why couldn't this stop?

'Who? What do you mean, sweetpea? Do you want to talk about it?' Shock flitted across his face even though he kept calm.

'What would *you* know? You're a man. What good is a *man* . . .?' No! That was a horrible thing to say.

Dad didn't speak then. I knew exactly what he thought I meant – that he'd never be as good as a mother – that I needed a mother and he wasn't good enough. His face was frozen, but I saw him falling apart behind it and my heart broke. I couldn't tell him that wasn't what I was saying. I couldn't even say I was sorry, no matter how loudly I was shouting it inside my head. Instead, my body took me swiftly upstairs where I couldn't see if he was OK.

I wish I could describe how I felt as I watched my life take blows like that right in front of me. It was one thing for me to upset my friends, but whatever this thing was, it was attacking my home now. It had come into the one place I always felt safe and loved. And I was helpless to stop it.

The hurt on Dad's face replayed itself in my head. I was desolate and furious – and physically numb and out of control – all at the same time. What tatters would be left of my life by the time I got my body back again? If I ever did . . .

In my room, I started opening drawers and taking out the contents in big handfuls, dropping stuff on to the floor and making a racket. I opened the wardrobe and pulled out all my bags, searching through for . . . well, I don't know. I was ransacking my own room – how crazy is that? I don't know how long I went on for, searching and destroying, but dusk turned to darkness outside my window. I lay down on the floor to get to the boxes under my bed. That's where I kept private stuff like diaries. But I wasn't me, so I had no right to touch them. It was like I was burgling myself – what *was* this?

As I watched my hands delve into those boxes and

start to look though my things, I started to get that feeling of rage again. At least maybe it was my own rage this time. There was no light to read the pages of my diary so I – well, my body – got up and moved over to the bedside table. My hand fumbled for the switch, further down the cord, my face right next to the bulb. When the switch clicked on, bright light burst through the blackness and flashed directly into my face and then I was rushing, zooming back into my body.

'Ye—!' I started to exclaim as knew I was back. Then I passed out.

Chapter 8

I could have been out for ten seconds or two hours. When I came round I just lay there for a moment, revelling in the feeling of moving my own fingers and toes. The feeling of the carpet as I moved my hands over it was crisp and clear and wonderful.

Huge relief flooded through me, knowing I wasn't gone forever – but the next wave to hit me was the horrible memory of everything I'd done in the last few hours. It was all a bit too much and I started sobbing. I cried harder than I'd cried for a long time and in the end I turned that light back off, curled up in my bed and kept on crying until I fell into a tormented sleep.

It wasn't until the morning that I started to really process everything. I'd been dreaming again but I didn't chase after the memories this time. I was too worried about the stuff that had gone on while I was awake.

This obviously wasn't a one-off fainting fit. And it obviously wasn't normal. I'd never heard anyone else ever talk about having any kind of experience like this before, so I couldn't imagine what else it could be – the only thing I could think of, other than that I must simply be going insane, was this TV documentary I'd seen about the way your personality can change if you have a brain tumour. I wasn't sure I wanted to find out that either of those things was wrong with me.

I thought about going to the doctor without telling Dad – and then I remembered what I'd said to him the night before. I buried myself deeper in my duvet at the shame of it and started crying again. I would never want him to think I'd rather talk to my mum when I was upset than confide in him. *He* was the one who'd stuck by me. He was a brilliant dad and I'd hurt him. My anger at myself rose up, thinking of all the times I'd taken him for granted, of every time I'd rolled my eyes at his clumsiness and every time I'd got cross with him for having trouble with those day-to-day things. I really didn't mind being the grown-up sometimes. It felt good to look after him. Besides, he let me be a child more often that I deserved. Whenever I was low or hurting, he was there, my gentle rock.

I couldn't believe I would do that, say what I said to him, even if I did have a tumour that was pressing on some essential piece of my brain. He was obviously hurt. He must have heard the noise from my room last night with all the mess I'd made in my ransacking episode. When I passed out he must have heard the thud and just assumed I was having a tantrum because he didn't come up to check on me once. How was I going to say sorry to him?

How was I going to say sorry to Anton and Gemma? I had actually hit both of them. Hard. This was going to be impossible to fix.

Instinctively, I wanted to call Katie. It was her last day at home before they went away but she'd still be there now – and she could always make me feel better. But when I imagined her picking up and saying hello, I couldn't do it. I remembered the looks on their faces when I tried to tell the Katies before. I'd hardly even *started* trying to explain and they thought I was crazy. I'd already made the decision that I'd have to go through this alone. The only way was to figure it out by myself.

I felt more alone than I'd ever felt. I'd always been happy with my own company, but I'd always been lucky enough to have someone to turn to when I needed them, too. Even if I did manage to convince everyone that something had taken me over and I hadn't known what I was doing; even if I could persuade the people I'd hurt to forgive me; how could I stop the whole thing happening again?

I clenched my fists, and scolded myself for thinking hopeless thoughts. If I was going to deal with this, I had to approach the whole thing scientifically. I was going to have to write down the times of my fits and work out if I could control it.

It only happened in the theatre. I could probably stop it ever happening again if I just didn't go back there. But we were practising hard and the next rehearsal was just a day away. As tough as I knew it was going to be, going there and seeing the others, having to say sorry to Anton, Gemma, Steve and David for messing up the last one, the thought of not going back was worse. Steve had said it was too late to get another Rebecca, so it wasn't just me that would be let down, it was everyone. Until that first blackout, the play had been the one thing I looked forward to. I couldn't let it all go that easily, I couldn't run away. I just had to be a grown-up about it, be brave and get in touch with everyone first to attempt these huge apologies. Maybe I could meet up with Gemma and have a proper talk before tomorrow's rehearsal.

I sat up and swung my legs over the side of the bed. As I tried to remember where I'd put my bag and mobile the night before, I caught sight of my face in the mirror and saw a massive, angry graze on my left cheek, close to my jaw. I must have hit the bedside table as I passed out. It hurt when I touched it and felt a bit swollen. How attractive. With all the scratches on my hands, the bruises on my legs and now this, I was starting to look like an extra out of *Fight Club*. At least my battered look matched the way I felt.

I found my bag and mobile under the bed where I'd been rummaging in those boxes the night before. But when I called to speak to Gemma, her mobile was off. When I called her home phone her mum said she'd gone out. I had a feeling she was ignoring me and had asked her mum to cover for her. I didn't blame her really, but it was frustrating when I really wanted to try to explain – even if they couldn't believe me. Anton's mobile was ringing out, so I sent them both a text to say I was sorry and that I really wanted to meet them before the rehearsal if they'd let me try to explain.

Feeling defeated, I scooched back into the corner of my bed against the wall and hid in a duvet cocoon. I stared at my phone, waiting for it to light up with a message. It didn't. Then I stared at the scribbled notes in my diary about when the blackouts had started and stopped. Wait! It was the same moment in the play that it happened – my first cue in the third act, the moment Rebecca discovers Tristan cheating. I'd been fine rehearsing up until then, both times. Maybe I didn't have to miss rehearsal completely. It wasn't the theatre that was making me ill. It wasn't even being on stage. It was that one moment. I could take control of this if I could just get Steve to skip that bit out.

I grabbed my phone and dialled.

'Hello?' It was good to have someone actually pick up the phone to me – even if it was nerve-wracking wondering how the conversation would go.

'Hi, Steve, it's Zoë. I'm so sorry about yesterday. I really honestly don't know what happened. I know that sounds stupid, but things have just been really . . . weird . . .' I blurted out as much as I could before he could say anything.

'Hello, Zoë. I appreciate your calling. You gave us all quite a shock, you know. Whatever's going on between you and Gemma and Anton, that was unacceptable yesterday. You know that, don't you?'

I wasn't being let off the hook easily. 'Of course, yes, I do. I am really sorry. I know there's no excuse but I've been feeling really odd lately – I've never done anything like that before, I swear.' I wanted to tell him that I'd fainted afterwards, at least then he might believe I was ill instead of just a violent crazy person. But I knew he'd tell me to go to the doctor – he might even tell my dad and I wasn't ready for that to happen yet.

'I can tell it's out of character, Zoë, that's why I haven't spoken to your dad about it – yet. But you're right, it doesn't make it OK. Can you promise me nothing like that will happen again?'

I didn't know what to say to that. Of course I wanted to just say yes, of course I did, but it's not like I decided to hit anyone last time – how could I guarantee it wouldn't happen again? I paused too long.

'Zoë, I need you to promise me.'

'I've honestly never hit anyone in my life before yesterday. It was horrible and I don't intend to let it happen again.' I held my breath, hoping that would be close enough to a promise.

'OK then,' he said. I exhaled. 'You've got another chance. Let's see how it goes tomorrow, shall we?'

Now I had to ask for the favour. I wasn't sure how to put it – I wasn't exactly in a position to bargain.

'Thanks, Steve. I'm going to do my best . . . Can I ask you something?'

'Sure.'

'This is going to sound really odd, but do you think there's any way we could avoid act three tomorrow? The start bit specifically. I know we obviously need to practise that bit, but I just think if we could leave it out tomorrow it might help things get back to normal.'

Steve was quiet for a minute and I couldn't guess what he was going to say.

'I can see why you don't want to do that scene and bring back memories of yesterday . . .'

Good, so it hadn't seemed like such a weird request after all. The question was would he agree?

'But it's probably the most important one, and we've only got two more practices really, even as well as you're all doing I'm not sure . . .'

'Please, Steve, I wouldn't ask if it wasn't important to me.'

71

'OK, Zoë, just this once, we'll miss it out. But this doesn't mean you don't have to deal with what happened, OK? This is just for one rehearsal. Whatever bad feeling there is, you need to get it sorted out quickly. Things aren't going to get put on hold for you.'

Yes. Thank goodness. I had some time.

'I know. Just this once is fine. Thank you, Steve.'

'OK. See you tomorrow. Five on the dot.'

'OK. Bye.'

Well, if all my apologies could go that well, I might just be all right. But I had a feeling they wouldn't.

Chapter 9

It was almost eleven a.m. and I wondered if Dad was in. I hadn't heard him. I lay down for ten minutes or so listening out for signs, and then I decided he must have gone out. So I figured I was safe to venture beyond my room.

I felt guilty trying to avoid him when I should have been seeking him out to say sorry, but it was sort of exhausting apologising – especially for things I hadn't meant to do – and I wanted to be totally ready to say what I wanted to say. I just really hoped he'd know, deep down, that I'd never mean what I seemed to mean when I'd said what I said.

There was a note in the kitchen: *Gone to the library at work. Back around four or five probably. Hope you're OK this morning . . . Dad x.* I touched the note where he'd signed off with an 'x' and it made me want to cry again. He was worried about me even though I'd been so horrible. I had to make sure whatever was happening to me didn't happen again. I couldn't stand to do this to the people I cared about.

I still wasn't sure how I could make a plan to stop something when I didn't know what was causing it, but I was going to do the best I could. I'd already made sure we were going to avoid the first scene of act three. What else could I do? The only thing I could think of was maybe I needed to get to the theatre before everyone else tomorrow and have a nose about. Maybe there was something on the stage that was making that dizzy feeling start at that particular moment.

I thought about that last spell and, of course, then I thought of my stagehand. I got that odd déjà vu feeling, where you know you've had a dream about someone but you can't remember what happened in it exactly. What I *could* remember was every millimetre of his face. Even though he'd been standing in shadow I knew the shape of him so well it wasn't healthy: his Adam's apple, full, soft mouth, clear, mesmerising eyes and cute nose . . .

He'd looked at me with shock, and then he moved forwards as if he wanted to save me and he looked so strong, like he could have, too, if something hadn't made him back off the way he did. Why did he back off? And, more to the point, how did he know I needed saving when no one else did?

I jumped up. I was such an idiot! It was obvious what I

74

had to do – I had to get to the theatre and find him. Why wait till tomorrow? I could find him now. I could look into those eyes again and find out his secrets – heat flushed my face at the thought. The theatre would be open and I couldn't sit doing nothing at home, not now I knew what I needed to do. I ran upstairs to shower and get dressed. I wanted to be fast so I pulled my hair back, threw on a T-shirt dress and trainer-style pumps and then rushed as fast as I could to the theatre.

I only slowed down when I got to that cocoon of trees around the theatre building; I was always a little awed by the cloak-and-dagger feel of walking up to it. I rushed up the steps and into the grand foyer. That cool, polished marble and that big circular design drew my gaze and held it. As I walked round the edge of the great room, I started to feel a bit woozy.

My heart leaped up into my mouth. Oh, wait.

Stop.

Was it happening again? Was I so stupid that I'd run headlong into a trap? I closed my eyes tightly. I breathed as slowly and calmly as I could. I counted my sensations – I could still feel my fingers, my toes . . . False alarm. Just a bit of plain old, ordinary dizziness. Rushing about on an empty stomach on a hot day will do that, I guess.

The ticket office booths were closed. The café looked open but was empty, except for one cashier who was hunched, unmoving, over a book. But I could hear the muffled, distant sound of piano music and singing. The doors to the auditorium were closed but as I got closer I could hear the voices more clearly: '*Follow, follow, follow, follow, follow-the-yellow-brick-road . . .*' I couldn't help a little smile. It was a rehearsal for *The Wizard of Oz*.

I leaned into the wall, feeling suddenly exhausted, not sure what to do next, my sense of purpose lost. How would I get in there if there was a rehearsal going on? I'd only ever seen the stagehand on stage. But now I couldn't get in there. Maybe I should have made a plan B. I wondered how long it would be before they finished – maybe I'd just wait . . .

Listening to the happy-sounding, melodic voices, I thought about what I might be doing now if I'd taken that part as second munchkin. I might be in amongst those voices, never knowing the fate I'd escaped.

Or what if I hadn't sat down next to Gemma in reception that day at auditions. I looked down at my still-scratched hands, which were shaking a little. I reached up to my face and touched the graze along my jaw. Still tender and swollen. Despite the battered, bruised state I was in, when I thought about going back to that moment, seeing Gemma sitting there jiggling about with nerves, trying not to chew her favourite dark red nail varnish off, I couldn't imagine not going over and taking that seat next to her all over again.

I couldn't turn back time. And I couldn't just hang

around waiting either – I wanted to find my stagehand *now* – and get some answers. What if I went round to the stage entrances? You could only open them from the inside, but they were quite often kept open so people could go in and out with props and stuff, or just go out for air between scenes when it was hot. But there was bound to be people milling about, too . . . Still, if they asked who I was, I could just tell them I was in one of the other plays and I'd left a bag backstage or something. Even if they watched me look for it, I could always just pretend to search and conclude someone must have handed it in.

Putting my plan into action was actually even easier than I'd imagined. The first door I came to was propped open and the few people I could see were all squashed into the wings, watching the action on stage. Tsk. Terrible security. Thank goodness. I stopped for a minute to scour the huddle of people, looking for him. But the only figure I could see wearing black was a woman with a tall pointy hat – not quite what I was looking for. So I slipped past unnoticed, ready with my lost-property line in case I bumped into anyone along the way.

I walked past the green room where everyone waits for their scenes. I hesitated for a second but figured I was likely to find *Wizard of Oz* people in there and have to explain myself. Besides, I'd spent plenty of time in there already and it was always full of actors – theatre staff didn't hang out in there. But there were four or five more rooms backstage I'd never been in. I wondered if any of them *was* a staff room, or if they were just props rooms and store cupboards. I could feel my nerves start to get the better of my determination. Even if one of them was a staff room, it wouldn't be OK for me to just walk in . . . Still, until I saw a door clearly marked *Private*, I figured I could get away with just playing dumb. My heart was thumping a bit as I moved towards a little corridor on the right.

That's when I saw him. Just a couple of metres away in front of me. He came right out of the corridor I'd been just about to turn into.

'Oh!' I called out before I had a chance to actually think of what I might say. I slapped my hand to my mouth in embarrassment but kept moving towards him. Then he turned round – and my racing heart stopped still. Oh my goodness. I wasn't ready for quite how stunning he was in the light of day. I sort of stopped and stumbled backwards, tripping over one of my own feet. I looked down at my clumsy, pale, freckly legs and regretted not wearing something nicer.

'Hi.' His voice was deep and resonant and lovely. I looked back up and he smiled at me, probably trying not to laugh, and the corners of his mouth curled up, making lovely little dimply creases in his cheeks.

I was breathing hard. Everything I'd been thinking seconds before dropped out of my head. I just stood there, unable to speak. How could I have possibly thought for a moment that I might have had a crush on Anton? *This* was a crush. When the whole of your insides turn to quivering mush. I had to gather all my strength to say something and I just ending up going into auto mode.

'I left my bag here the other day – I'm in one of the other plays – I'm just trying to find it,' I blurted.

'I know. I've seen you rehearsing. You're good. It's a good play too. I've had fun watching you all.' What did he have to go and compliment me for? Just to add to his impossible loveliness and my deepening blush. I knew I was supposed to be here looking for answers, but I honestly couldn't think of what the questions were I was supposed to ask now I was here, face to face with him.

'Oh, thanks.' I looked down at my shoes because looking into his pure blue, searching eyes was too much for my pulse. I'm too young to have a heart attack. When I looked up he'd come closer. I really thought I might pass out. I was actually, literally, swooning.

'Do you know where you left it? Your bag? I'd help you look, but I should get back to the lighting desk really . . .'

'Oh, you're doing the lighting for *The Wizard of Oz*?' A question! Getting straight to the point there with an incisive question, Zoë. Smooth. Good thing I decided to come backstage after all, because the answer to this could solve all my problems . . .

'I'm just assisting really, I'm a sort of apprentice. Actually, the guy lighting this one, Roger, he's very serious.

He won't even let me touch the board yet. But I just like being here. I love the buzz of it, you know?' I did know – he felt just the same as me.

'Yes! I do. I really do,' I gushed as I stared at him, desperate to say more but utterly sidetracked by just looking. His eyes danced as he thought about being in the theatre and his smile just took my breath away. The shape of his shoulders and arms through his short-sleeved black shirt made me tingle . . . Behind me I could hear a couple of actors coming off stage, chatting in whispers.

'Well, I should go,' he started. Damn it, damn it. Argh! I couldn't think of anything else to say to keep him there. He seemed a bit jumpy suddenly. 'But listen, erm, I can't – don't have a pen, but leave your number at the office and if your bag turns up I, someone, will call you, OK?' He was already turning away but he gave me another dimply smile. I nodded and smiled and muttered thanks as I watched him go round the corner.

Gah! I'm so useless. I didn't ask *anything* I was supposed to. Not even his name. I'd been incapacitated. He was more amazing-looking than anyone I'd seen before. But ignoring my stupefaction for a moment, what was I meant to say? Nice to meet you. So, did you see me not-quite-pass out on stage the other day? When you looked at me did you stare into my soul at all? Because it seemed like you did.

Wait – did he ask for my number though?! He said to

leave my number. Was it a bit psycho-stalker-ish to take that as him asking for my number? I figured probably yes. But I had to leave my number now, even though I hadn't actually lost a bag. Was it wrong to pretend I'd lost a bag so I could leave my phone number in the tiniest hope it might somehow mean he'd ring me?

There must have been a break then, because people started to flood backstage. My instinct was to hide. I ducked down the corridor he had come from. Maybe I could come back and leave a bag somewhere for real, and *then* leave my number . . . I looked for somewhere I could hide it. The first door I tried was locked, which meant I obviously wasn't supposed to be back there. I glanced around. No witnesses. I wandered a bit further. The second door opened nice and easily with no telltale creaking and I went in. There's wasn't much in the room except boxes. What was I doing? Sneaking around looking for somewhere convincing to leave a bag I'd lied about losing in the hope a guy would find it and call me . . . Argh! I was going mad. It wasn't like he was actually *asking for my number* – a guy like that wouldn't be asking for my number. It was ridiculous. I had to try and snap out of this.

I could still hear a lot of chatting outside so I stayed and nosed through the boxes. Some looked like they might be new deliveries – paint and tiles and stuff. Others though, especially in one corner, were full of old, dusty stuff – loads of assorted old props. Once it was quiet enough, I turned to leave, but something flashed, on the edge of my vision. I spun back round, my heart thumping, and there was a mirror. It must have just caught the light. I laughed and rolled my eyes at myself. Talk about jumpy.

I went over to the mirror – it was quite big, just the corner of it was sticking out from the box and it was half covered in a dust sheet. It was heavy, but I pulled it out of the box and lifted it up. My face was too close up for me to really see myself. But I saw the woman standing behind me.

I'd been caught.

I yelped, a strangled scream, dropped the mirror and spun round.

There was no one there. I caught my breath and swallowed hard. There was a hat stand behind the door I hadn't seen and there were a couple of old costume jackets hanging on it. My nerves must have been making me see things.

But I was so sure there'd been a woman there. I'd seen details. Her long, raven-black hair and pale skin. I'd even noticed her eyes – striking green – because she'd been staring at me, hard. How would I imagine all that from a hat stand?

Maybe it was a trick mirror or something. I turned back and crouched by the mirror. Thank God it hadn't smashed. Feeling a bit sick and woozy again, I propped it up, pushing it back to an arm's length away, so I could look properly. There was no one in the mirror but me. I looked at myself.

It didn't seem like a trick mirror. I stared at my face. And as I looked, my normally grey-blue eyes suddenly glowed bright green.

I gasped a breath in so hard it hurt. Scrambling backwards across the floor away from the reflection, I was shaking and terrified. That was no trick – what the hell was happening to me?

I squashed myself as hard as I could into the corner of the room and just sobbed with horror.

As soon as I could get my shaking legs to work, I got out of that room. I rushed past the green room to the door and out on to the street. Then I ran and ran.

Chapter 10

Dad was still out when I got home. I went straight to my room – I wanted to hide from everything. I drew the curtains and covered my mirrors. There was no reasonable explanation for what I felt so sure I'd seen – I must be turning insane.

I wanted Dad to come home. I wanted to sit with him in the kitchen, over dinner, and tell him everything. But part of me still couldn't bear to face him because I felt so guilty. Another part of me was angry that I felt guilty for something I didn't feel like I'd done of my own free will. I wanted to believe someone was plotting against me somehow, because otherwise it meant there was a side of me I suddenly couldn't control.

I wrote Dad a note: *Hi Dad. I'm so sorry I was horrible last night. I didn't mean anything . . . I'm just not feeling right at the moment. I'm getting an early night to sleep it off. Love you. Z xx.* I ran downstairs, stuck the note to the fridge, grabbed a stash of food, and got upstairs again as quickly as I could.

I lay awake in bed with the light off. I heard Dad come in and make food in the kitchen. It made me smile to hear him crashing about. I thought about going downstairs a few times, but there was so much noise in my head that I was too exhausted. Despite all the serious problems I should be thinking about – like what did I really see in that props room? What could I say to Dad to make him forgive me? What was I going to say to Gemma and Anton tomorrow? (I hadn't heard back from either of them) – the thing that kept taking over all my thoughts was my conversation with the stagehand. I cringed at how embarrassing I'd been, but his smile had just left me helpless. He said he'd seen me and that I was good. He had actually said that. But he was probably just being nice.

I decided I'd text Gemma once more. *Really honestly sorry. Want 2 come tomorrow but wish you'd meet me 1st. I'll b in the café half hr before practice. Pls come.* Then I tried to read for a while but I soon realised I was just staring at the page.

Dad said once that mad people don't know they're mad. So even if I was having these weird fits and hallucinations, if I concluded I must be insane, because insanity was the only sane conclusion, then my conclusion was sane – and that proved I wasn't mad, right? Argh!

As I drifted away from consciousness I even started thinking maybe someone might be poisoning me. I started making a mental list of everything I'd had to eat or drink and who might have had access to it. I think it was about one a.m. when I finally fell asleep properly.

I woke up suddenly and nervously about nine hours later to the sound of the back door slamming. I'd had more dreams but I didn't want to remember them. I didn't open my eyes. I just lay there, moving my toes, my legs, my torso, my arms – wondering if I'd sustained any new overnight injuries. No pain. But when I stretched out my fingers, they felt sticky – just the first two fingers of my right hand. I sighed and slowly opened my eyes, edging my hand out from under the duvet. They were shiny with bits of fluff from my pyjama bottoms stuck to them. I tried to wipe them clean with a tissue from my bedside drawer but the stickiness was pretty stubborn. Then I recognised the fruit smell of my favourite lip-gloss, which Katy had given me on my last birthday.

I rubbed my eyes with the backs of my hands and went over to my dressing table. The scarf I'd used to cover my mirror was lying on the floor and, smeared across the reflective surface, in big capital letters, were the words: *MARION KNOWS*. I actually stood there open-mouthed. This was ridiculous.

It didn't look like my writing. Not that I'd ever written in my sleep before, so who knows. But I didn't even know anyone called Marion! Who the hell was Marion?

I didn't know whether to laugh or scream so I just swore disbelievingly for a bit. That was really nice lip-gloss too. And expensive. And there was hardly any left now. This stuff just got weirder and weirder. I really didn't know what this meant. And I didn't know which I felt the most: fear, confusion, anger, or anxiety about the day ahead. I was on edge the whole time while I showered and dressed and went to the theatre.

Gemma was late. I was just staring into the dregs of my coffee, wondering how long to sit and wait before I gave up. Then she appeared. I smiled at her, taking her arrival as a good sign, but she didn't smile back. She looked away as she sat down. My heart sank but I was determined I wouldn't go to pieces.

'Thanks for coming. I wanted to say sorry properly before rehearsal. I really am. I don't know what happened – I really don't know what made me do it. I think there might be something really wrong with me. Ever since I fainted that day, it's like I haven't been in control of what I'm doing . . .' I'd thought about this apology over and over. It had never sounded so weak when I'd said it in my head. Gemma still wouldn't look at me and my throat had dried up.

'Is that it?' she asked quietly, putting her bag over her

shoulder as if to leave. I didn't know what to say. I guess my speechlessness made her angry because she looked at me then. For a couple of seconds anyway. 'I'm sorry, Zoë. But just think about what you're saying, honestly. If I told you I had some sort of illness that made me punch people in the stomach or slap them in the face, would you believe me? It's obvious this is about me and Anton. I *did* ask you. I gave you the chance to tell me the truth, but you were clearly lying when you said you were OK with it.'

No! She had it all wrong. 'I am. I *am* OK with it, I *swear* . . .' But what else could I say? She was right. You don't hit someone and then say, 'Oops, sorry, it wasn't my fault.'

'I'm sorry,' she repeated, 'but I'm not ready to forgive you for this yet. Let's just be civil for the sake of the play for now. OK?'

And that was it. She walked away. I felt tears welling up and knew I had to get away too. But I didn't want to follow her out of the theatre – she'd made it clear she didn't want me chasing after her. So I went through to the auditorium. Thankfully, the doors were open and it was empty in there – and dark, to suit my mood. I sat in the back row, clutched my bag to my chest like it was a comfort blanket and cried.

'Are you OK?'

I let out a little scream as my heart jumped. It was him. The stagehand. Oh. Good timing.

'God, you scared me. I didn't see you there.' The

nerves pounded in my stomach, seeing him standing there – butterflies doesn't describe it, quite. Wild horses, maybe . . .

'Sorry. If you want to be alone, I'll go . . .' I nearly kicked myself for snapping at him. But why did the most stunning guy I'd ever met want to speak to me *now*, when I was a wreck? But of course I didn't want him to go. Now he'd already seen my stupid blubbing face anyway, what I really wanted was a hug. I wanted him to wrap me in his arms. I wondered what he smelled like. Oh my goodness, snap out of it.

'No, no, please, it's fine. Sorry. It'd be nice talking to someone who doesn't hate me for a change.' I wiped my face dry and moved my bag from the seat next to me and on to the floor. I gestured for him to sit, but he took the next seat along. I tried not to feel snubbed. It was sort of gentlemanly, I suppose.

'Are you OK? You look awful,' he said.

Oh, this was going great. I couldn't help laughing at that, which actually made me feel a lot better. 'Thanks!' I smiled at him and he grimaced.

'Sorry, I didn't mean that the way it sounded.' He smiled the cutest, shy smile back at me. 'I mean you look sad. And hurt. What happened to your face?' He pointed at the graze on my cheek. I'd forgotten about it and instinctively reached up to cover it, even though, clearly, he'd already seen it.

'I fainted on to my bedside table. I seem to be having a lot of dizzy spells lately, although that's actually the least of my problems . . .' I looked at him, and he was looking back at me, his big, clear blue eyes focused completely on me, a worried little crinkle between his eyebrows. Just sitting there with him, a wave of calm came over me, like I was safe. I thought I might tell him everything then. It felt like such a long time since I'd confided in someone. Time seemed to have stopped still, like we could talk forever if we wanted. But if I actually told him everything, he'd think I was crazy. Violent and crazy. And I didn't even know his name.

He broke away from my gaze, looking down at his hands, fiddling with his fingernails. He had really nice hands. When he looked back at me, it was through his eyebrows, a sort of almost guilty look. It took me by surprise.

'What is it?' I asked, not really meaning to ask out loud.

'I wanted to tell you something.'

My heart leaped at the thought of what he might be about to say, and I cursed my overactive imagination.

'But I didn't want you to think I was weird . . .' Oh, it probably wasn't a declaration of love then.

'That's funny,' I said. 'I was actually thinking something pretty similar.'

'I think I know what's happening to you.'

That left me stunned. For a second I thought I'd misheard, but his eyes told me he'd said it for real and he was serious. He looked right at me. My heart was racing again, only now everything was sharp and clear, like his words had been a blast of cold water in my face.

'What?' I murmured.

'I wanted to tell you when I saw you yesterday, but it's not the sort of thing you open a conversation with when you don't even know a person's name.' He smiled his curly smile at me again. 'I'm Jack, by the way.' I half expected him to offer his hand to shake, the proper way he spoke. But his hands were clutched tightly around his ankle, which was folded up on to his knee in that awkward-looking square, leg-crossing thing that men do.

'I'm Zoë. Hi.' I smiled back and looked directly and unblushingly into his eyes for the first time. 'Now that we're properly introduced,' I urged quietly, 'please tell me what you mean.'

'I was watching you at rehearsal the other day. I think you saw me?' I nodded. I knew it! I knew he'd seen there was something wrong. 'There was someone there, behind you.'

I got a cold, creeping feeling.

'Who?' I breathed. My head was so full of questions but I didn't want to interrupt – he was obviously finding it hard to explain what he'd seen. He seemed worried I'd think he was deluded or something, but I was just desperate for answers. 'Please tell me. Believe me – nothing you could say would sound as weird as what I've been feeling.'

Chapter 11

Jack turned to face me more directly.

'A woman. A pale woman with long, black hair . . .'

'And green eyes!' I finished, holding my spinning head in both hands.

'Yes! You've seen her?' I think Jack was excited I'd had proof of what he was saying. I was excited too – as well as sick – there *was* someone doing this to me. I *knew* it wasn't me.

'Who *is* she, Jack? What's she doing to me?'

'I'm not completely sure – I've never seen anything like it before, but she . . . stepped into you.'

Every hair I had stood on end. Hair I didn't know I had stood on end. I was reeling.

'She was standing behind you and she looked furious . . . She got closer to you and I stepped forward, not thinking.

I could see that you could feel it – in your eyes. I could see you were scared and that you could somehow feel her coming. And then she just . . . stepped into you. Your eyes went blank for a second and then they were hers. They had the same anger in them. I didn't know what to do. I'm sorry.'

'Please don't be. I'm so glad you're telling me this, you have no idea – I honestly thought I was going mad.'

'I promise you're not. It's not you.'

'She's . . . a ghost, isn't she?'

I couldn't believe the words that were coming from my mouth, but there wasn't a flicker on Jack's face.

'I think so.' He nodded.

He didn't think I was crazy. He trusted me. And I trusted him. Even though he was telling me something that just a few weeks ago I wouldn't have believed for a second.

'I don't believe in ghosts.' I laughed softly, looking up at the stage and feeling clammy to the stomach. 'The funny thing is, in the general scale of weird things that have been happening to me, this actually doesn't seem that weird at all. In fact, it explains things perfectly. And it's a massive relief to know I'm not imagining it all, or dying of a brain tumour.'

'I thought you'd think *I* was insane if I tried to tell you what I'd seen.'

I shook my head as he smiled at me. I knew he was telling me exactly what he saw. There was no way he could be making it up – because I'd seen her too. And I'd seen her eyes in mine, just like he had. I thought I might throw up, thinking about it. I covered my mouth with my hand and hugged my stomach with my other arm. This was all mad.

'Are you OK?' His voice was deep and soft and soothing. It had a calming effect on me, like the rumble of a train carriage along its tracks.

'Yes. I'm sorry. I'm just trying not to be sick. It's a lot to take in but I'm so glad to know what's happening . . .

'Why couldn't anyone else see her?' I wasn't really asking him. It was more that I was just thinking how unfair it all was that none of my friends would ever believe this.

'I'm different.' He shrugged, staring down at his hands again.

'I guess so.' I looked at him until he met my gaze. 'Have you seen ghosts before?' I asked suddenly. I couldn't hide the wonder in my voice. He looked back down at his hands and I realised he was wondering again how much he could tell me.

'Yes,' he confessed, exhaling. 'Never like this though.' I felt, in a way, like he was as relieved as I was to talk about this with someone. This explained why he seemed so quiet and alone. He had a secret no one would understand. After the last few days, I knew how lonely that felt.

'That must be hard . . .' I half stated and half asked, curious but not wanting to pry.

'Sometimes.' He shrugged. 'Other times it has its up

sides.' He looked at me and smiled again. He was so lovely I couldn't help staring again as I smiled back. We were quiet for a few moments as we looked at each other.

It felt like we were connected, like we were both alone except for each other. Maybe it was wishful thinking that he felt the same connection I did.

A slow, amused smile crept on to his face. 'You didn't leave your number yesterday – I checked at the ticket office.'

'Oh.' I blushed, embarrassed at remembering our awkward conversation and my lies, but also secretly thrilled that he'd checked. 'I got distracted. That's when I saw her, the ghost, she was in the mirror in the props room . . .'

Jack nodded, trying to be serious, but the smirk crept back. 'I couldn't find your bag I'm afraid, but I was going to let you know I'd looked.'

I flushed red again and winced. 'There's no bag,' I confessed. Why did I have to do that? Why couldn't I just say thanks and keep quiet. I just couldn't keep secrets.

'I know.' Jack grinned a brilliant grin and my insides somersaulted. My jaw dropped a little and he laughed the most irresistible laugh – I had to remind myself he was laughing at *me*. I managed to recover enough to shoot him a scowl for being so devious. He just laughed harder and although I tried my hardest I couldn't stop myself smiling.

Then I remembered real life. It was only a few minutes

until I was supposed to start rehearsal. I went quiet and then Jack did too.

'I'm being possessed by a ghost,' I said, nodding to myself in disbelief. It sounded ridiculous to say it out loud. 'The others could be here any second. I'm supposed to get up there and act. I don't know if I can. I mean, apart from the fact everyone hates me – she could be there, waiting for me. I don't think I can go through it again.'

'So go. You still have time to get out. Go now.' There was urgency in his voice. He jumped up, ready to let me out. But I didn't move. I thought about my last conversation with Steve. He'd given me another chance. And he'd promised me we'd avoid *that* scene, even though it was a really important one to rehearse.

'I can't.' I almost whispered it and closed my eyes, I just felt so defeated. 'As scared as I am, I'm on my last chance with this play. If I don't do this, I'm out. I'm not ready to throw it all away yet – and for some dead person I don't even know, who picked me to mess with for some reason . . . I really don't want to have to go up there. But giving up now would be worse.' I stared up at the stage.

'You're right.' Jack was nodding again when I looked at him. 'You've got more guts than me, but you're right.' There he went again with his compliments, catching me off guard. 'I was surprised when you came back, after the first time . . . I was glad you did.'

My heart sped up and I flushed with heat yet again; he

could render me useless when he said lovely things like that.

'It's not bravery at all,' I argued. 'It's fear. I'm too scared of losing what I care about. Who I care about.'

'Fighting for what you care about? That sounds like bravery to me.' He wouldn't let me reject his compliment.

I can't tell you how much I wished that he would just take me out of there then, take me away so I could just be with him instead of facing the horrible afternoon ahead.

'Zoë, listen.' Oh, he said my name. I'd never heard my name sound so good. 'I'm going to stay with you.' He'd read my mind. Oh wait – he was a mind reader as well as seeing dead people? I really hoped he didn't know what I was thinking about him. That would be *mortifying* . . .

'I'm going to stay, through your rehearsal, and I'm going to watch you. But you have to watch me too, OK? Because I'm going to be looking for her. And if I see her, I'm going to signal like mad at you and you have to get out as fast as you can.'

As he told me his plan, he was already backing out of the row of seats to let me through. I wanted to hug him – this was brilliant – not only would he have my back, but I'd have a friend there too, to see me through the horrors of rehearsing with people who hated me.

'Do you think it'll work?' I asked, my excitement starting to bubble.

'It took her a good few seconds before, I think, to . . . do what she did, as if it took work to build up to it. I'm sure if she turns up again you can get away in time. And then, if I can see her – maybe I can talk to her. Maybe I can find out what she wants.'

I was practically jumping with anticipation. If this could just work . . .

'You think she wants something? From me?' It hadn't occurred to me to think about what might be driving her. I'd been more interested in me.

'She's angry. Something's tying her to the theatre. I'm sure she wants something – whether we can work out what, I don't know, but if we can, maybe she'll move on.'

I loved the way he was saying 'we'. Like there was no question that he was going to do all he could to help me.

'Thank you,' I said, taking a step towards him.

He backed off.

'We should be quick.' He tried to disguise his step backwards as a glance towards the doors, but I'd spotted it. 'I should get up on stage and hide,' he said, starting to move round the back of the auditorium. 'I should keep hidden as much as I can if I'm going to be a lookout. Just look for me as soon as you start, OK?'

I nodded as he headed down the other side of the seats, to the curtained entrance at the side of the stage. What he was saying made perfect sense but I felt a bit bemused about the way he'd backed off, like he didn't want me near him. Until then I'd felt we were getting on so well.

I grabbed my bag from the floor and by the time I

looked up he'd gone. Steve arrived literally seconds later, so I guess Jack had been right to rush off. I went straight out the back to help Steve bring some of the props out. It was good to be busy when the others got there. It meant I didn't really have to interact with them until we were in character.

Before I even made my first entrance, I spotted Jack hiding in the wings on the other side of the stage. David was there too, pushing his floppy fringe out of his eyes as ever, deliberately avoiding eye contact with me, and then with just a curtain between them, there was Jack, grinning stupidly, giving me a thumbs-up. I smirked at him. He made me feel like I could face anything.

The first act went OK. I was tense – I hadn't spoken to Anton since the incident – but relations were supposed to be tense between our characters so it worked OK. I'd glance at Jack when I could, and he'd give me a nod and a smile to let me know I was OK.

Then we spent most of act two, which I wasn't in, looking across the back of the stage at each other while the others acted. Jack kept an eye on me the whole time, checking behind me, even though I could see he wanted to watch the scene too, that he loved being in the theatre. Whenever we'd catch each other's eye he'd smile his lovely smile at me. I felt like there was electricity running though me. I told myself it was the danger I knew I was in, and the thrill of trying to outwit it. But I think it was as much to do with just being with Jack. Every time our eyes met it was delicious and exciting and like being wrapped in a soft, warm blanket all at once. I felt invincible.

Until Steve betrayed me.

'OK. Great, guys, great. Act three then!'

What?! I came out from behind the curtain.

'Oh, Zoë, I know we spoke before about skipping this, but it's been going so well – let's give it a try, OK? Tristan and Diana, can you bring the chaise longue through?' It seemed that was the end of the discussion then. What the hell did he think he was doing? He promised me!

I was fuming but I had no choice except to go back to where I'd been standing. I was terrified. My stomach had the floating horror you feel as you go over the top of a rollercoaster.

I hadn't told Jack about this part of the play, that she always came at that moment. I looked at him and the terror on my face obviously told him for me. He frowned and looked questioningly at me as he stood to attention.

I held my hands over my mouth and started to cry. I couldn't bear to have this happen to me again. Jack looked panicked, but he was peering hard behind me and still giving me the OK sign. The scraping of props along the stage stopped and the acting started. I watched Jack closely, keeping eye contact, still clutching my mouth closed.

'We've got hours and hours, all to ourselves . . .' I heard Anton purr. I stepped forward just as Jack's eyes went wide and urgent – he started waving wildly at me to get off the stage. I screamed and ran to the front of the stage, practically breaking my neck as I slipped jumping off it, only just recovering my balance.

'Zoë!' Steve screeched.

'Sorry, sorry, sorry! I really have to pee!' I screeched back. It was the only thing I could think of as I ran for the back of the room, grabbing my bag as I burst out through the doors.

I ran to the ladies', just off the foyer, and locked myself into a cubicle where I sat on top of the toilet seat, hugging my bag and my knees. I was frozen with fear. Should I still be running? What if the ghost was chasing after me? She could be just on the other side of the door . . .

Chapter 12

'Zoë? Are you OK?'

It was Jack. I was still in the cubicle. It took me a minute to come to my senses. I flexed my fingers and my toes – I could feel them just fine. I touched my hands together and I touched my face. Everything worked. I was breathing hard, and shaking, but I wasn't dizzy or queasy . . .

Ha! We'd done it! I stood up on the seat and looked over the top of the cubicle door at him and, when he saw I was OK, he grinned.

'We did it, didn't we?' he said.

I nodded excitedly and then glanced around. 'Jack – this is the *ladies*',' I told him with pretend shock.

'I won't tell if you won't.' He shrugged with a cheeky smile.

'You're so *naughty*,' I said.

'I've had my moments.' He twinkled his eyes at me and waggled his eyebrows. I nearly fell off the toilet he was so gorgeous. 'Now come down out of your tower, princess, and I'll meet you outside.'

'OK.' I grinned at him and jumped down. I took a second to catch my breath, leaning against the door, before I slid open the lock. I was in love. I was sure of it. What a time for it to finally happen.

Outside the door, Jack was leaning against the wall with his hands stuffed firmly in his pockets. I looked around and into the foyer to see if anyone might be listening, but we were sort of screened from the main area by a curved wall that sectioned off the bit where the toilets were.

'I'm shaking,' I said, holding my quivering hands out in front of me and leaning against the wall close to him.

'You're safe though,' Jack reassured me. 'It was the weirdest thing, Zoë, but when you jumped down off the stage, she couldn't follow you. I watched it. She tried to go after you, but when she got to the edge of the stage it was as if she couldn't go any further . . .'

'She's definitely been past the edge of the stage before, she's been out of the theatre – in my house even . . .'

'But that was when she was with you, *in* you, right? So my guess is that she can go wherever she likes when she can keep holding on to you, but otherwise she's stuck in that tiny space somehow. But you're her ticket to the outside world, Zoë, and she'll do anything to get out of here. I

104

could see the fury and determination in her – you can't go back up there on that stage again right now, it's too dangerous.'

I secretly liked that he sounded like he was telling me what to do – not that I was going to take orders from anyone, no matter how stunning they were. But it made me want to kiss him, the way he looked so worried about me, the way he was working so hard to protect me. I stared at his lips, imagining what it would feel like. I wanted to move closer to him, it was taking a lot of will power not to. But last time I tried it, he'd backed off . . .

'You have to get out now, while you can.' His voice interrupted my thoughts.

He'd been right so far, but I didn't know if I could do what he was asking. Despite our triumph, I was still stuck in the same dilemma.

'If I wimp out of this now, I'll get chucked out of the play – it'll get cancelled completely. I don't know if I can do it.'

'Zoë, I know this is important to you, I understand, really, I love this place too, the whole magic of it . . . but this is bigger than that; we're talking about your *life*. Look at what she's already done to you.' He nodded at the big ugly graze on my face. I couldn't believe I'd forgotten about it. Maybe that was why he was keeping his distance from me. Because I looked so hideous he didn't want me to touch him. All the excitement of our victory was draining out of me fast.

'Is that it then? I have to give everything up? She's beaten me – so close to opening night? We only had two rehearsals left.' I turned away from Jack and stared at the floor, ashamed and broken.

'I'm not talking about quitting altogether, I'm just talking about now, while she's waiting for you up there. You just need to stay safe until we can figure it out. Look, if your director admitted he'd have to cancel the play without you, if you don't have an understudy and it'd be too late to get another Rebecca, that's all the more reason he's likely to give you another chance, right? He did the last time, and let's be honest, last time was a lot more, um, *interesting*.' He shot me a guilty grin and I shot him back a glare. 'All you did this time was run away.' He was right. Steve wouldn't really cancel the play completely, not if he could avoid it, not now.

'Maybe you're right. He did break his promise to me too – he said we could miss that scene out and he went back on his word. Maybe he'd feel bad if I called him on it . . . but so what if he does agree to give me another chance? For what? To get possessed again? Going back up on that stage just gives her the chance to get me again. What's the point?'

'Zoë . . .' Jack's voice was so compelling, so gentle and strong all at once, I had to look at him, hideous face graze or no hideous face graze. 'Don't give up. Ducking out of this rehearsal doesn't mean giving up the whole play. We haven't got a plan yet, but I really think you need to find out what she wants and maybe we can get rid of her.'

I wanted to believe him. 'How can we find anything out by running away?'

'She must be in this particular place for a reason. Perhaps you could read up on the theatre's history. When's your next rehearsal?' Jack asked, resolve colouring his tone.

'Monday night.'

'Can you do some research – in the library or something? There's two days till then . . .'

'I can search online – my dad's a media studies teacher, he has access to newspaper archive sites, I can try using those . . . but what use will that be?'

'I'm not sure. Perhaps, we can help her.'

I felt a pang of anger. 'Why would I want to *help* her? She's ruined my life.' I pouted. I knew what he was saying made sense, I was just letting myself wallow.

'Something must be keeping her here. If we can work out what, maybe she'll go – cross over, rest in peace, whatever. It's worth a try, isn't it? Come on. I know you're not ready to give up. You've got more fire in you than that, I've seen it.' This boy sure knew how to say the right things – I felt amazing when he said stuff like that.

'OK. I'll go home now and see what I can find. Why don't you come with me?' I surprised myself asking him that, but I just didn't want to not be with him. The thought of leaving without him made me feel horrible.

His face fell, showing me all too clearly the answer to

my question. 'I can't. I don't get off here until seven, and I'll have to wait till then before I can do any digging, or I could get caught . . .'

I tried not to show how much I wanted to cry.

'OK. Well, what's your number then? I can call you and tell you what I've found.'

He looked at me blankly for a second. 'But I'll be here.'

'Oh, I guess you're not allowed to have your mobile on while you're working. I could call you after though.'

'No, it won't work. I mean it's broken. The only phone I have is the payphone in my digs – it doesn't take incoming calls because the landlady's a battleaxe . . .' He laughed nervously, rolling his eyes. I felt actual pain in my chest as he started backing off again. 'But look, leave your number at the ticket office, like you were supposed to before, OK?' He raised his eyebrow in mock disapproval, but I could tell he was hiding something, his nerves showed through. 'I promise I'll try calling you as soon as I can. But I should get back to work – and you *should* go – before they come to look for you. We've been talking too long.' And then he was rushing off across the polished floor of the entrance hall.

I watched him disappear into the shadowy corridor by the auditorium. I couldn't believe he'd run off again. What was going on with him? One minute he'd say the loveliest thing to me and the next it was like he couldn't stand to be near me. I was full of confusion as I headed quietly in the opposite direction, creeping towards the box office and the exit, making sure I avoided accidental contact with the others. I didn't think any of them apart from Steve would be searching too hard for me.

I still felt a tiny bit wobbly from the fear of how close I'd been to the ghost – and the thrill of escaping. But mostly I felt rejected. When Jack and I looked into each other's eyes, it was like there was no one else in the world. He smiled at me like I was the only person he saw, just like Anton had with Gemma. It was what I'd wished for. But it was like he held my heart in his hand just to break it. All I did was ask for his phone number and he acted like I'd proposed or something. Whenever I tried to get closer to him, he ran away. Pretty much literally. I didn't understand him at all. I'd be so sure he liked me and then so sure he didn't. Why did this have to be so confusing, on top of everything else? I scrabbled in my bag for a pen and scrap of paper, wrote my number down and posted it through the ticket window of the closed box office. I had no idea if he'd call me. I took one last glance around and left the theatre. There was no way I was going back on that stage knowing she could be there waiting for me. Not until I had a plan.

Coming through the front door at home I felt a little thrill to be me, you know, without a ghost on board. And even though I couldn't get Jack out of my head, I tried to focus on the research I had to do. If Jack was right and knowledge was power, I could really do with knowing some more stuff.

I went straight to the study and flicked to the back of dad's diary. He was so terrible at remembering passwords and log-ins that he kept a list of them all there. I'd told him off for it, saying that if we were burgled or something, it'd be the perfect way to help someone hack into his bank accounts and steal all his money and his identity. But right now it turned out handy for me. I'm sure he would have let me use it if I'd asked him anyway, but that could mean a lot of explaining I didn't know if I could do.

I searched for *Hemingford Theatre*, all records, but that turned up hundreds of thousands of results and it was just listings mostly. I wasn't sure how to narrow it down. I didn't even know what decade to look under, really. This woman could have died any time . . . so I put *died* in the narrow search field.

That was easy – when the results came up I only had to weed out a couple of obituaries of old actors before I found this headline from the local paper: *Fatal Accident in Local Theatre May Have Been* Foul Play. I clicked on it and read the full article. It was dated 1960.

Two people were killed on Saturday night in seemingly unrelated incidents at the Hemingford Theatre, Cooper Mews.

It was definitely our theatre.

Actress, Olivia Brett, 21, and a theatre technician,

Christopher John Bloom, 19, were both rushed to hospital but both died from their injuries. Miss Brett, who was starring in the production, Foul Play, *was fatally wounded in what appeared to audience members to have been a stunt gone tragically wrong . . .*

It was the same play! This had to be it.

As theatre staff rushed to help the actress, Mr Bloom was discovered unconscious with head injuries. Police are working to discover whether either incident did indeed involve any foul play or whether these were simply two tragic accidents.

That was it? I needed more information than that! I went back to the headlines and found a later article.

Stage Shooting Was Accident, the title read. I clicked through again. *Olivia Brett, the 21-year-old actress shot and killed on stage at the Hemingford Theatre last week, was not murdered, police have confirmed.*

My heart thumped fast in my chest – this was creepy. She was actually killed on the stage – it must have happened in act three – when Tristan shoots Rebecca. Only she was shot for real and actually died right in the middle of the play? How could that happen?

Detectives have dismissed speculation that the prop gun, used in the Foul Play *production on Saturday, may have been deliberately swapped with a genuine, live weapon, as salacious hearsay.*

Whatever that meant.

Miss Brett's co-stars, Thomas Garvey, 24, to whom the actress was engaged to be married, and Marion Sylvester, 23, were being questioned in connection with the incident but have been released without charge.

MARION! *Marion knows*! I remembered the sticky message on my mirror. My mouth went dry and my mind began to race. This must be it – I've found it. These people were all in the same play as me, nearly fifty years ago. Olivia was obviously playing Rebecca and Thomas and Marion were the only other actors mentioned in the article, so they must be playing Anton and Gemma's parts.

I had to be close to the answer but I still didn't have enough information. I ran an image search on the names and found a picture of the whole cast, with the director, on the steps of the theatre. Then I knew for sure. My eyes were drawn straight away to the striking woman in the centre with long black hair and pale skin. A chill shot through me. It was a black and white photo but there was still no mistaking those eyes.

I checked the caption. It was her. I'd seen Olivia Brett in the props room. Forty-eight years after she'd died. I felt hot and sick. I ran to the bathroom and vomited.

All of this was real.

Chapter 13

I sat there on the bathroom floor, my hot, spinning head resting against the cold wall tiles. I'd been relieved when Jack told me what he thought was going on. I was being possessed by a ghost. It was an answer, finally, and proof that it wasn't me doing all those horrible things, that it wasn't my fault. But now that I had a name and I really knew it was true, I wasn't sure if this wasn't worse – I had no control over this, and no one could help. They wouldn't be able to *believe* me, let alone help.

Then Jack's words echoed in my head. 'Maybe we can get rid of her.' If we could find out what she wanted, maybe we could beat her. If I could focus on *her* instead of thinking how hopeless things were for *me*, maybe I could keep going.

I gingerly pulled myself up on to my feet. Cold and

shaking, I went back to the computer screen. After a few deep breaths with my eyes closed, I looked at the picture again. When I looked at Olivia I noticed this time how gentle she seemed. She was smiling a warm smile, so different to the angry face I'd seen. She didn't seem evil at all. Thomas was standing next to her and their smiles both seemed so real and comfortable. He was classically good-looking, almost beautiful, with his soft, dark hair swept back carefully in a sort of quiff. He was tall and tanned but sort of baby-faced. Next to him was Marion, who was also beautiful, but in a completely different way to Olivia. Marion had a shock of bright blond curls, a small, heart-shaped face and delicate features.

Olivia was striking, grown-up looking and elegantly beautiful. Marion, even though she was older, was more girly, a sort of pretty beautiful. On the other side of Olivia in the photo, according to the caption, was the director: Richard Sylvester. It was obvious he and Marion were related, probably brother and sister. Although Richard's blond hair was carefully tamed with shiny gel or oil or something, you could see the curls didn't want to submit. He had the same delicate, neat features Marion had, but on a very manly, big face with a huge Buzz-Lightyear-type chin. He was good-looking too, in a sort of US-football-jock way. They were all good-looking, even Ted McClean, the man on the end, next to Richard. He was older, with dark hair that was speckled with grey just around his ears, but he was still sort of dashing, a bit George Clooney. I figured he must be the bit-part actor, like David.

I must have been staring at that picture for ages, in a sort of trance, because when I heard the door slam, it made me jump. And I realised how little light there was in the room beyond the glow of the screen. It was almost dark outside.

'Zoë! Are you there? I've just had a call from Steve,' said Dad, throwing open the study door. You know he's cross when he doesn't say hello, he just gets right to the point. 'He says you ran out of rehearsal, right in the middle, with no explanation – what sort of behaviour is that?'

'I'm sorry, Dad, I was ill. I've just been sick.' I was pretty sure I still looked quite rough from throwing up and I hoped that'd be enough to get me out of trouble. Dad switched on the light and I couldn't help shrieking as I squeezed my eyes shut against the brightness.

'You do look pale,' admitted Dad. 'But if you're ill you should be resting, not playing on the computer. Besides, don't think I don't know this isn't the first time you've been misbehaving at rehearsals. Steve wouldn't even give me the specifics of what else you've been doing to disrupt things – what's going on with you?'

'I'm sorry, Dad, I just haven't been feeling well, that's all.' I knew it would sound like a pathetic excuse. Thank goodness Steve hadn't told Dad everything, or I'd have had to come up with something much better. 'And I will go and rest in a bit, I promise, I just have to finish a bit of research for Monday . . .'

'It's not me you have to apologise to, is it? Even if you're ill, you have to explain to people – you can't just run away like a child.'

He really meant it. I could tell he was frustrated with me and I felt guilty about it. But I couldn't explain the truth, could I?

'You've got ten minutes. Then I want you to call Steve to apologise and go straight upstairs and lie down. I'll bring you up some soup in a bit.'

As soon as he'd gone I turned back to the computer. I looked through a couple more articles but couldn't find anything with any more detail. There was nothing about how the real gun got on stage – all the articles were really vague about the inquest, just declaring it an accident, case closed. So I tried entering all their names in new searches and that was more helpful. I found out Thomas and Richard had both died, Richard in a boating accident in 1978 and Thomas after a drinking binge in 1983. The articles I read confirmed Marion and Richard were brother and sister, and that Thomas had developed a *difficult relationship with alcohol*, whatever *that* was supposed to mean. I don't know why they didn't just say he was an alcoholic.

I found Ted's name in a few theatre listings, the latest being in Cardiff in 1980, and one listing for Marion, a

116

marriage announcement: Marion Elise Sylvester to Terence James Goldworthy, 15 December, 1966.

So, Marion's last name would probably be Goldworthy now. That got me thinking. I opened a new tab and brought up a directory listings site, searching for local M Goldworthys. Man. I was good at this detective stuff – there were only three in the local area: a Mark Goldworthy, an M F Goldworthy, who was listed as a company director and one M E Goldworthy. Marion Elise. That was her, it had to be. I'd found her. I tore off a page of Dad's telephone pad and wrote down the address. When I put the postcode into a map search I saw it was only about half an hour's walk away, if I took a track that cut across the fields.

'Your ten minutes are up!' shouted Dad from the kitchen, so I shut down.

In my room later, I stared at the scribbled address. Could I really go and see this woman? Just turn up on her doorstep? What would I say?

I jumped when my phone rang next to me. I'd just finished my awkward conversation with Steve about two minutes before, so it was lying quite close by when it sprang to life. I'd been miles away, staring at that scribbled address, propped up with the bowl of half-eaten soup.

I put a hand to my chest and laughed at my own jumpiness. But it had freaked me out. *Number unknown* said the screen. I hesitated. I don't usually answer those calls. But this time I did.

'Hello?'

'Zoë?'

'Jack!' I didn't manage any hint of cool – it was like a shot of adrenalin to hear his voice.

He laughed. 'You seem surprised to hear from me. I *said* I'd call . . .'

I felt a twang of annoyance. 'Yeah, but you were pretty much running away from me at the time, so I wasn't sure if you were just saying that for an easier exit.'

He was quiet for a second. 'I'm sorry if it seemed that way. It was only that I realised how long we'd been standing there – I didn't want your friends to find you and take you back in there . . . I'm sorry if I seemed off, honestly.'

It was my turn to be quiet. I had to give him full marks for a sincere apology.

'Did you get home all right in the end?' he continued.

'Mmhmm.'

'So come on then, tell me what you found out. I know there's something, I can tell.'

How did he *do* that? I couldn't keep quiet, it was so good to be able to talk that I couldn't waste time being mad. I went into high-speed mode.

'It's Olivia Brett. That's her name, the ghost. She played the same part as me in the same play in 1960, but she died on stage – she was shot. You know the bit when Rebecca gets shot? Well, it was a real gun. The police thought that maybe someone had swapped it. She might have even died right there, on the stage we've been walking on every day. It's no wonder she's tied to that spot.' If Jack was about to react, I didn't give him a chance. 'And Marion, the other actress who was there, the one that played Diana, I've got her address – it's only about half an hour's walk away. I could so easily go and see her . . .'

'Wow, you've been busy! You should be a detective – are you sure?'

'I know!' It was freaky to say it all out loud, it was such a terrifying story, but I was excited at how much I'd found out. 'And yes, I'm positive. I saw a picture of the cast, it's definitely her.'

'What picture? Who was in it?'

'The cast. Marion, Thomas, Olivia and Ted. Oh and the director, Marion's brother.'

'That's it?'

'Yes, why? It was definitely her, Jack, I'm positive. I couldn't mistake her face – I can print it out and show it to you . . .'

'No, no, I believe you. What I meant was, are you sure about going to see the other actress?'

'I don't know.' I sighed. 'I mean, I know it's going to be hard to know what to say – it's not like I can just walk up to her door and say, "Hi – did you used to know Olivia Brett? Because I'm the girl her spirit is haunting, and this is going to sound weird, but she says you know how she died" . . . but I have to think of *something*.'

'Zoë, you have to slow down.' Jack laughed. He sounded serious and soft but like he couldn't help being amused by my gabbling. I blushed with embarrassment and tingled at the same time, from the sound of his laughter. I lay back on the bed, one hand over my face even though he couldn't see my blushing from the other end of a phoneline. I sighed again, this time feeling myself relax. He had such power over my mood.

'I know. Sorry. It's just so good to be able to talk about this. I thought I was completely alone until you . . .' I tailed off, not wanting to say anything too much.

'You're not alone, now, Zoë, I promise. As long as you need me . . .' He tailed off too and my heart thumped hard at the thought he might want to say more as well.

'Thank you, Jack, I don't know why you're being so sweet to me.'

'It's not difficult,' he answered gently.

I played with the corner of my pillowcase, just enjoying knowing he was there. It occurred to me I couldn't picture where he was.

'Hey,' I said softly, 'where are you calling from, by the way? That funny payphone?'

There was a pause and he coughed away from the receiver. 'Excuse me. Urgh, yes I'm calling from the funny payphone.' His voice cracked a little and he cleared his throat again. 'The landlady's such a miser – I'm sure she's got it wired up illegally or something – she's so worried about it costing her money somehow. And it's ancient – I'm surprised it even works at all. But listen, Zoë, I'm not sure about you going to see this woman.'

'But it's what Olivia wants,' I argued, urgency creeping back in. 'You were the one who said we should do what she wants. I didn't tell you, she wrote on my mirror the other night, the night she came home with me, or maybe I wrote it in my sleep but I'm sure it came from her: *Marion knows*. In big letters on my mirror.'

'I said we needed to *find out* what she wants, not necessarily that we should *do* it. I think there could be more to this than what's in the papers, that's all – there's some stuff you can't print without proof.'

'Wow, that's cryptic.' I was starting to get frustrated.

'Sorry,' he conceded. 'It's just you said the gun might have been deliberately swapped – if it was, that's murder. You could be in dangerous territory . . .'

'But the police investigated it and they decided it was an accident.'

'That doesn't mean they didn't still have suspicions, it just means they didn't have the evidence to prove them. Who did they question, did the paper say?'

'Thomas. And Marion,' I said sheepishly.

'So she was even a suspect! And you were happily planning a visit to her house?'

'Jack, just because she was questioned, it doesn't mean

she was a suspect.' I was arguing but I was starting to feel that maybe he had a point. 'She was just there at the scene – that's like standard procedure or something, right? What motive would she have to kill Olivia?'

'That's what I mean – all we know is what was in the paper. She could easily have had a motive we don't know about. Maybe it was a crime of passion. Did you find out anything about their love lives?'

I got a crawling feeling in my stomach.

'Olivia was engaged to Thomas. The male lead.'

'Ha!' said Jack.

I couldn't help smiling at his glee, even though he was clearly winning the argument now.

'So, maybe Marion wanted Thomas. Or, they were questioned together you said? So maybe she already had him. Maybe they were having an affair and they wanted Olivia out of the way.'

'That's a lot of maybes but, wow, if it was true, it would certainly explain why Olivia's so peed off. That'd be nasty. But why would they kill her? Why couldn't Thomas just dump her and go out with Marion?'

Jack shrugged. 'Maybe Olivia just found out about the affair and went a bit psycho. Maybe she threatened to kill Marion – or Thomas – or both. And so they killed her in self-defence – or, at least, in advance of having to do it in self-defence.'

'Erm, OK. So what you're saying is I'm not only being

haunted, I'm being haunted by a psycho nutter? Great.'

'All I'm saying is be sure, before you go to see Marion, that it's what you want to do . . .'

'Jack, she's the only lead we have. She's the only person I can think of who can really give us any answers beyond what we've been able to find out on our own.'

'But, Zoë, think about it. The *reason* she might be the only person left who knows what happened is because she might be the one who killed her. She could be a murderer. If you stir this up you could be putting yourself in danger.'

I shivered. He was right, but I didn't know what to say. I still had a strong feeling that this was what I had to do.

'The thing is, I think I'm sort of in danger *anyway*, aren't I?' I felt weirdly calm as I tried to explain. 'If not of death, then of losing everything I care about. I can't think what else to do.'

'Please don't go. At least give me a chance to think of a way to keep you safe first, OK? And I'll meet you on Monday, before your rehearsal. Will you promise?'

'OK,' I sighed.

'I don't like hearing you sound so sad,' Jack whispered.

I hadn't realised it was so obvious but he always seemed to be able to read me easily. I swallowed hard against the feeling of wanting to cry.

'I wish I had an answer for you. I wish there was something I could do to help.'

123

'You already are,' I told him. 'Honestly. If it weren't for you, Olivia could be sitting here right now instead of me – I wouldn't have got away from her.' I closed my eyes. 'And just being able to hear your voice. You have *no* idea how much that helps.'

'I'm glad,' he said. I turned to look at the space next to me and reached out to touch the empty duvet. What used to just be air was now so wrong, an aching absence of what – who – should be there.

'I wish you could be here,' I whispered, holding my breath, dreading as the words came out that I'd said too much.

'Me too. You have no idea.' He echoed my words. He didn't sound as if I'd freaked him out, he sounded like he felt the same way. But I was sure it was too much to hope for – someone like him, and someone like me, an average girl with stupid freckles and a haystack for hair. I put my hand up to it and sure enough it was already forming into bedhead clumps . . .

'If I could reach over and touch that hair, and your face, just once . . .'

I felt faint as his soft whisper reached me. It felt like the phone wasn't there, like he'd whispered in my ear from just a fraction of a millimetre away.

' . . . I could go to sleep happy,' he finished. I couldn't move or breathe or feel my toes.

We were both silent for a moment. And then he said just

what I was hoping he wouldn't.

'I have to go.'

I exhaled shakily.

'I'm sorry. I wish I didn't have to. But I'll see you on Monday, OK? In the auditorium, at five?'

'Yes,' I murmured. I didn't know how I was going to wait so long to see him.

'Goodnight, beautiful Zoë.'

'Goodnight . . .' I could barely get the word out. After another second the line went dead.

I couldn't believe it. He couldn't mean the things he'd said, he couldn't really feel the same . . . could he?

Chapter 14

I opened my eyes and the wooden planks of the stage stretched out in front of me. Rows and rows of empty seats seemed to stare at me. I couldn't move.

A syrupy, dark red liquid began to ooze out in front of me. Suddenly there were faces in the auditorium. They were all laughing at me. Jade and Jenni, then Gemma and Anton. As the mocking cast grew larger, David and Steve appeared, then Katy and Katie . . . Dad . . .

I couldn't understand. Everyone hated me. Everything hurt. Then I was being lifted effortlessly. I heard Jack's voice, so soft in my ear.

'I don't like seeing you so sad.' A thrill ran through me as I felt his mouth brush lightly against my ear and then against my neck. I closed my eyes. 'You're not alone now, Zoë.'

I felt a breeze against my face and when I opened my eyes I saw Jack staring back at me, smiling his beautiful, curly smile with the dimples, his eyes twinkling at me even in the shadows. All around us were leaves, glowing green as the moonlight shone through them. In the spaces between, I could stare into inky patches of night sky, deep as forever and punctured with stars.

Where were we? I felt around me, my fingers finding rough bark. I could smell the woody, leafy smell and the summer sweetness in the night air – it wasn't like a dream at all. But then I looked around us again and saw the roof of the theatre. I gasped. We were sitting in a tree. I turned sharply back to face Jack. His smile broadened into that breathtaking grin.

'It's OK, Zoë, you're safe.' And it was true, the branch beneath us was sturdy, and there were more all around and below us to steady against. I felt soothed and totally secure. Then my stomach churned suddenly, as I remembered the blood – I looked down at myself, expecting to see red . . . but I was fine.

Embarrassment quickly replaced my relief and I blushed a burning red, suddenly very aware of being in my pyjama bottoms and vest top, my hair was probably one big tangle. He reached up towards my face and I inhaled sharply again, my pulse thudding as the tips of his fingers touched my forehead. We were close enough that I thought I heard his breath quicken too. He gently pushed my hair away from my face and tucked it behind my ear. Then he reached up again to the top of my head, smoothing his hand downwards, his touch still gentle but stronger this time. I could feel the strength and size of his hand against me as it stroked down over my hair into the crook of my neck. That grin flashed across his face again and he chuckled quietly.

'I love your crazy hair,' Jack said, giving up trying to smooth it down.

I flinched with embarrassment but couldn't help laughing too – his was so infectious. As we laughed together, warmth soothed my electric nerves. He put his hand down on the branch so his little finger just brushed against mine. His shoulders squared up as he shifted his weight a little to face me. As he relaxed again, my eyes followed the muscular line of his shoulder, along the curve of his neck and his jaw. I couldn't resist the longing in the pit of my stomach. I reached out and put my hand on his face, feeling the contrast between the stubble-shadowed skin of his face and the smoother skin of his neck. I stretched towards his mouth with my thumb to touch his lips.

His eyes closed for a moment and he smiled very gently. Barely aware of it, I leaned towards him. As his eyes opened again he leaned too until his cheek brushed mine. I felt the heat of his lips brush closer to my mouth and I stopped breathing. Then our lips were together, just touching at first. I wound my hand around the back of his neck. He held my face, threading his fingers into my hair. We both leaned into our kiss. As he held on to me more tightly, his lips were stronger and more urgent. A shuddering sigh shook through me and I woke up.

I was desolate and alone in the darkness, still clutching my pillow, desperate to retrace my steps back into sleep but knowing the memory of where I'd just been would keep me awake for hours. I was stunned at the strength of the sensations. I'd never had a dream like it. I closed my eyes and traced my mouth with my fingertips. The touch of his lips had been so real.

For most of the weekend, I was Dad's prisoner. He worked in his study all day instead of going to the library and, every time I came down from my room, he'd pop his head out and check what I was doing. He insisted I 'rest up and get well' but I knew he just wanted to keep me where he knew what I was up to.

My mind was filled with that dream, the horror of its beginning completely obliterated by Jack – and that kiss – if I closed my eyes I could still feel it. In the light of day though, I was embarrassed at the heat of my imagination. I must have been kissing my pillow in my sleep for it to feel so real.

The thing was, it hadn't *all* been fantasy, had it? I had my doubts, after such a vivid dream, but I had to remind myself that he'd said lovely things to me in reality, too. Did he honestly say he wanted to touch my hair and my face? Did he really call me beautiful? I'd find myself grinning thinking about it. It was probably a good thing I wasn't being allowed out of the house – I'd have just been walking around blushing and grinning madly and making a fool of myself.

I tried to watch TV but all I could think about was Jack. Over and over and over, and then when Olivia began to creep into my thoughts, I thought of Jack again. Not just because I wanted to see his face and talk to him and just be with him, but because I needed him too – I had no plan and I was scared.

After the high of escaping Olivia, and then finding out who she was and what happened to her, after unearthing all that information, I was still defenceless. Once I was back on stage tomorrow, there was nothing that could protect me from her except running away again.

It made me feel all clammy and hollow, thinking of the way she used my body like it was a mug for her tea – a vessel she could use however she chose. Now, when I looked down at my hands or I looked in the mirror, I saw someone different. I wasn't completely me, there was something alien in what I saw. You get used to your body. No matter how flawed you feel it is, you begin to take it for granted. But when it suddenly doesn't feel like it's yours any more, everything changes.

Olivia knew just enough about me to invade my life. She

knew my lines – that's how I'd got through rehearsal without anyone realising it wasn't me. She knew where I lived. But what did she want from me? Revenge? Justice? If she was murdered, maybe she wanted me to avenge her death. Or maybe she was just plain angry that she was dead and didn't even know what she was doing. Even if she *did* know what she wanted, was there any way I could find out? I could hardly talk to her, could I? Because as soon as she turned up she claimed ownership of my mouth.

Should I risk it and try and go to talk to Marion? I'd promised Jack I wouldn't, and to be honest, it was a relief.

'Zoë?' I jumped as Dad shouted from the hallway on Sunday morning. 'I'm going to the shop for a paper and some milk – why don't you come with me and get some fresh air?'

I knew why he was asking and it wasn't to do with fresh air. I felt sad as I shouted to him that I'd get changed and be down in a minute. I missed how we used to be – more like a partnership than father and daughter. It was horrible feeling like he didn't trust me any more. I couldn't wait until tomorrow, when he'd have to let me out to go to the theatre.

That evening, I got a brilliantly long email from Katy. It was a welcome distraction and it sounded like they were having the best time, getting up late, lying on the beach for the afternoon, getting chatted up by loads of lads, going back to their apartment where their parents had cooked dinner – and then back out in the evening to the cafés on the waterfront. Katie had written a bit at the bottom too, in the same email. It was so sweet of them to remember me, and Katy wrote in so much detail it almost felt like I was there with them. Part of me would have given anything if I could have been. Another part of me wouldn't trade the last few days for all the holidays in the world. Because, despite all the terror and frustration I'd been through, I wouldn't want to give up that excited flutter I felt knowing that, in less than twenty-four hours, I'd see him again.

Chapter 15

When I peeked through the doors of the auditorium, he was sitting there in the same seats where we'd talked before, waiting for me.

'Ah, there you are.' He'd turned and smiled that curly smile at me when he heard me come through the doors.

'Hey,' I answered, smiling broadly back. My stomach flipped and I flushed red again as I sat next to him, I couldn't helping thinking of that dream. I closed my eyes, trying to push the sensations out of my mind – the tingle of our skin touching, the warmth of his lips brushing my cheek – I couldn't have a conversation with him if my head was full of that.

'Are you OK?' He sounded a little sad as he asked.

'Mmhmm,' I said, biting my lip. I turned to look at him and couldn't help an embarrassed grin. 'I had a dream about you.' Gah, I couldn't *believe* how rubbish I was at not saying stuff out loud.

He smiled, sending me into palpitations. 'Oh reeaally.' He raised an eyebrow at me.

'You know how it is,' I tried to backtrack, 'when you dream about someone, and then you see them and it's sort of funny . . .'

'Was it a funny dream?' His smile softened.

After a moment I shook my head. 'Not really, no. Not funny . . .' I said quietly.

'I had a dream about you, too.'

My insides flipped – yet again. 'Oh rreeeaally?' I grinned again, arching my eyebrow back at him. 'What was I doing in yours?'

He pursed his lips for a second in the cutest guilty expression and I laughed. 'I'm not going to tell you anything. It was . . . nice.' He smiled at me again and I was sure I could hear my heart thudding in my chest. 'If yours was nice too, let's not spoil it by describing them? We could pretend we had the same one.'

I just nodded as I looked at him, because I couldn't speak.

After a moment, he looked away, suddenly seeming upset. 'I'm so sorry, Zoë. I feel horrible. I hoped once we got here and were sitting together like this that I'd have a plan. I made you promise not to go to see Marion, but now I don't have any answers. It's only a few more minutes until your rehearsal starts and you're facing the same danger as before

– I don't know how to protect you. If I could think of anything, I swear, I'd do it . . .'

I felt a wrench in my chest to see him look so sad.

'I'll let you into a secret,' I offered. 'I didn't want to go and see Marion anyway. I was too scared. Promising you I wouldn't was just the easiest way of chickening out. Besides,' I added, 'it's not up to you to solve all my problems. I don't exactly have a plan either.'

'We'll just have to do what we did last time.' He looked at me sadly again as he shrugged. 'But, chances are, you'll have to run off stage again.' He was right. I barely noticed him stand and edge towards the aisle. 'I'll get up there now. Look for me as soon as you're on stage?'

I smiled weakly at him and nodded. I gathered my bag to go backstage while he disappeared.

I was just dropping my bag in the green room when Anton and Gemma walked in. I don't know why shock turned my stomach – I knew I'd see them – they just caught me off guard and I froze.

'I need a drink,' Gemma said to Anton as soon as she saw me. 'Let's go to the café.'

Anton obediently turned and followed Gemma straight out of the room. Neither of them would even look at me. I felt a weight on my chest and had to slump on to one of the sofas and steel myself against tears.

All I could do was try my best to keep going. To get back up on that stage and just wait while Jack played lookout for me again. My palms started to feel clammy as I thought of Olivia getting me. But we'd beaten her once. We could do it again.

'We've got hours and hours completely to ourselves . . .' came Anton's line.

I got ready to walk on stage, trying to keep my breathing regular, trying not to panic. I looked at Jack. He was nodding and giving me an OK sign. Knowing he was watching meant I could go on.

'Why . . . Rebecca, darling . . . I thought you'd left over an hour ago. I . . .' said Anton.

'So it seems. Well, I'm sorry to disappoint you, Tristan.' HA! That was me! I stole a glance at Jack, hope surging through me. *I* delivered that line. Alone! Jack was smiling his kissable, curly smile and nodding as I carried on, his eyebrows were raised in encouragement.

'I'll give you an hour to pack your things . . .' I went on. Could that be it? Maybe, just maybe, it was over. I was getting to say my lines with Anton for the first time in what felt like a really, really long time.

Could it be possible that Olivia just wanted me to find out about her story? Could it be that she just wanted me to know what happened to her? Maybe, once I'd read those newspaper articles, that was enough to satisfy her?

' . . . or it might be more than adultery you're charged with when I get my lawyer on to this.' I finished my line and, high on my own sensations, I turned back to where I'd come on, ready to take Tristan's bullet.

As I heard him fumble in the prop sideboard behind me, it suddenly made me think how horrible it must have been that night – when Olivia was killed. I shivered. Everyone in the audience would have been watching, thinking how convincing it was as the bullet went into her. They probably gasped at the realistic blood that seeped out, thinking how impressive the stage make-up and effects were. And the shock on her face as she spun round and fell down – what fantastic acting . . . How long must it have been before the realisation had started to spread through the crowd – that it was real?

The thought of it made me feel dizzy. I could see it all happen so vividly, I felt sick. I heard Steve pop the balloon to signal the gunshot and I spun round, throwing Tristan that fleeting look of shock and anger before I collapsed, just like we'd rehearsed. Falling on to the hard wooden stage, I thought I'd seen Jack waving . . . I heard him shout my name just too late . . . just as my vision started to blur and darken.

Olivia was clever. She'd learned from her mistakes, just like me. This time she'd waited until we'd let our guards down, until my back was turned and I couldn't see Jack. She'd stayed hidden until I was lying on the stage, unable to run away when Jack shouted his warning. And then she got me.

It might sound weird but after the panic of it, when I realised she'd taken over, the horror of it didn't feel so strong this time. I knew what was happening to me and I knew who was doing it. A part of me even thought that at least I'd actually get though the rehearsal without having to run away again.

When Anton and Gemma carried me off stage at the end of that scene, Jack was waiting. He stalked over as I got up. He looked at me – well, Olivia – angrily and, while the others were moving the chaise longue, for a moment we were together, hidden in the shadows of the wings.

'Olivia, you leave Zoë alone,' he hissed. 'You're destroying her life – it's not fair.'

'Don't tell *me* about fair – just don't even get me *started*,' Olivia growled through my gritted teeth, turning back to help the others move the props.

It was so strange to have Jack talk to me as Olivia, and when I spoke back, knowing he knew I wasn't me. It was horrible to have him look so angrily at me, I hadn't seen him look like that before. But he was still beautiful, even with fury in his expression. And I had to remind myself he was angry because he wanted to protect me. He was angry at Olivia because of what she was doing to me.

But there was nothing he could do. Olivia had walked away and was setting up with the others for the next scene. She glanced back at him for a moment, shooting him a warning glance. He was fuming but just watching. What could he do? He couldn't continue the conversation with Olivia with everyone there. To him I was Olivia but, to them, I was Zoë. If he tried to speak to her, it wouldn't make sense to anyone – he'd seem crazy. She was safe while she was there on stage with the others, and she wasn't going anywhere – at least not until our tea break, when she went right out of the theatre, taking me with her.

So much for getting through a rehearsal finally.

'Hey Zoë, where are you going – you OK?' David called after me. He was smoking outside the theatre as Olivia rushed me through the doors and down the steps. He was on his own because Gemma was making Anton quit. It was so wonderful to hear him speak to me, they'd all been so careful not to. It was like he'd decided to make an effort to reach out to me.

But as soon as I felt a gleam of hope, it was gone – Olivia turned around, looked him up and down, and then without a word, turned back and kept on walking. It was about as damning a snub as you could get. I wanted to scream and scream at her. How *dare* she? What had I ever done to her that she could do this to me? I didn't care what she'd been through – it was just plain evil. I needed Jack. Where was he? He'd made me belive we were in this together. He made me need him – and now he'd left me alone.

It took about fifteen minutes of walking for me to realise where Olivia was taking me. It was when we took the track across the fields that I knew. She was taking me to Marion's house. I couldn't understand how she knew where to go, unless she used my memories and thoughts somehow, like they were files on a computer she'd hacked into – or, unless she had been with me all the time . . . that even when I got my body back, she was still with me in some way . . . In that hypnotised state I was all too familiar with by now, I watched as Olivia took me through the kissing gate at the other edge of the field and out on to the road that led to Marion's cul-de-sac. It must have been well past eight p.m. by then, because it was getting dark.

I watched her bang on the door with my fist and I was terrified of what she might do. Being careful clearly wasn't something she was bothered about. I guess life's too short to worry about that sort of thing when you're dead. But if she thought it was Marion's fault she was dead, she might do anything – and if she was right, so could Marion.

I don't know how much of my own rage was coursing through me and how much of it was Olivia's. But if Olivia had been alive and standing in front of me right then, after all this, I wondered if I'd have been angry enough to murder her myself.

Everything was dark and still despite Olivia's banging. I prayed Marion was out, not just asleep and about to wake up – or worse, hiding and terrified, about to call the police.

If the police came and I was arrested, would I have a criminal record for the rest of my life? Causing a public disturbance? Assault? I'm sure Olivia was willing the hall light to come on, for the light to shine out suddenly through the glass panels of the door, for a human shape to appear in the hallway. I was willing it not to.

Chapter 16

Another few minutes passed and nothing happened. It seemed I was safe. For now. Olivia crouched down on the floor and rifled through my bag, finding my notebook and pen. I had to watch as she wrote a vicious note with my hand.

You won't get away with murder. You might have killed me, but Rebecca has come back to life – and she'll have her revenge for what Tristan and Diana did to her – you know what happens in the last act. Your only hope is to confess now – before it's too late.

The last act? That's when Rebecca realises she's going to die in the cellar. It's the middle of the night and, knowing her cheating husband and his mistress are asleep upstairs, she decides that if she's going to die in her own house, she'll take them with her. She gathers the gas canisters in the cellar and starts a fire . . . Was Olivia threatening to burn down Marion's house – while she was still inside?

I couldn't believe she was going to post it, but the moment she'd finished, she stuffed the note through the letterbox, lacerating my finger on the tightly-sprung metal flap in the process. This mad woman wouldn't be satisfied until I was either in hospital or jail.

Hospital or jail. I know it's crazy, but when I thought about it then I started considering throwing myself down the stairs or something, the next opportunity I got. Hospital was better than jail – and at least if I was laid up in hospital that would limit the damage she could do to my life. I wouldn't be allowed to go out – I might even be sedated. I was even visualising it, lying in a bed with broken bones in casts and not able to move, before my reason kicked in. I realised with anger that this dead woman had already left me scratched, grazed and bruised. Now she was making me *want* to hurt myself as well? I wouldn't give her the satisfaction. If I was going to beat her I had to stay strong. She might want to destroy me but I wasn't about to *help* her.

There was a great rumble of thunder as we moved away from the house and back on to the road. By the time we got to that gate again, it was raining quite hard. Big, heavy drops hit the overheated pavement. I longed to smell it and feel the moisture in the air and the drops on my skin, but I was engulfed in Olivia's dark, numbing cage. She marched us home and, while the sky darkened, the track across the field got squidgier with mud at every step.

We got to the house and she got in through the back door using my key. She headed straight for the stairs. She didn't even stop to think about taking off my dirt-caked shoes. Even in the almost-dark I could see her trampling great, wet splodges of mud and grass all over the hall carpet with my ruined shoes. I couldn't work out if it was rudeness to the point of disrespect or just plain madness – but, every time I thought she'd reached the last straw with making my life miserable, she found one more way to make things worse.

Then I heard Dad's car pull into the driveway. Olivia stopped still in the doorway, looking out through the window of the front door, but he wasn't in view yet. I heard him get out and slam the car door. I heard the jangle of his keys. Then the security light in the porch flicked on with a sudden, bright flash. Olivia let out a little yelp, then there was that familiar, welcome rush and then blackness.

I had just come round and sat up on the hall carpet when the main light clicked on too. Having carefully unlaced and removed his shoes in the porch, he was now faced with dirty great clumps of mud stamped into the carpet anyway.

'What the hell are you playing at, Zoë? Have you seen this mess? And you left the back door open and you're soaked through – and why are you creeping about in the dark?'

'Erm . . .' I really couldn't think of an explanation. 'I passed out . . .'

I saw Dad's face flicker with concern for a second, but this clearly wasn't the best time to confess everything.

'Well, you certainly didn't ruin this carpet while you were passed out, that's for sure. I've had a long day, Zoë, really long.' He put his briefcase down and rubbed his face – he did look wiped out. 'I just wanted to relax with a drink . . . I can't handle this now. I'm going out for an hour or two. I want you to do the best you can to clean this up and I want you to think very carefully about what the hell's going on with you lately because, frankly, I can't. I give up trying to figure out what's going on in your head.' He turned back into the porch, shoes still in hand, and shut the door loudly behind him.

The words rang in my head: 'I give up'. I knew he only meant just for now, this minute, not for ever, and I know kids have done way worse things than ruin a carpet. But I felt totally deflated then. I couldn't bear it that Dad didn't like me any more.

I felt so angry and so alone, scrubbing and dabbing at the floor. And, on top of everything, I couldn't get Jack out of my head. The one person I'd be able to talk to about Olivia and everything she'd done to me that evening and I couldn't get in touch with him. I felt hurt that he hadn't come after me when Olivia took me out of the theatre. He said he wanted to protect me. He said that if he could think of anything to help he'd do it, but then something as simple as following to see if I was OK he wouldn't do? I was starting to think what he said and what he did were two very different things.

My thoughts fuelled a growing ball of anger inside me. And what was it with this whole phone arrangement anyway? He must be lying about his mobile being broken – you'd just get a new one, or get it fixed, wouldn't you? Everyone has a mobile. Even Katy's ten-year-old little sister had one.

In my mind, I could see his smiling face and the thumbs-up signal he'd kept giving me. My anger sank away as I remembered the feeling I'd had, knowing he was watching over me, ready to give me a smile whenever I needed it – I'd felt safe, happy, excited. Like I mattered. Like I was beautiful even. Then I thought about how little I really knew about him and how defensive he got whenever I got too close to him.

Why did everything have to be so hard?

I'd just laid my head on my pillow when my phone rang again. This time I didn't have to pick it up to get that electric thrill. I leaped to answer.

'Jack?'

'Zoë? Thank God you're OK. I couldn't find you – you *are* OK?'

'Yes, I'm OK.' I'd been so angry with him still, but in a second he had me again, the concern in his voice was obvious.

'I'm *so* sorry. She came out of nowhere and your back was turned – and she wouldn't listen when I tried to speak to her – then at break time I lost her. She left from the other side of the stage and by the time I got to the front she was gone . . . Did anything horrible happen?'

I couldn't understand how he'd lost sight of me so easily, but it was obvious he was upset.

'Don't worry, it wasn't your fault – I let my guard down too. It was all deliberate – she knows what she's doing, she knew I wouldn't see your warning if she waited until I turned away. I heard you call out, but it was too late. It doesn't matter now. Anyway, you'll never guess where she took me: Marion's.'

'Oh, *God*,' Jack groaned. 'What happened?'

I told him about the note, the new injury and the hallway carpet. 'For better or worse, I guess she took the decision out of my hands about talking to Marion. I can't go back there now. That was a pretty crazy note – crazy enough to get me into serious trouble. And if I went to see her now, and tried to explain what's happening, it'd be obvious it was me that put it through her door. She said about Rebecca coming back to life, and as far as I know, I'm the only incarnation of Rebecca around right now. I'm not going to give her the chance to call the police on me. No, all I can do now is keep my head down and hope she doesn't do anything with the note or find out about the play and who I am.'

'You really think you'd get in trouble for that? Just a note?'

'Yes, I think so – there was a proper threat in there.' Then something occurred to me. 'Besides, after what I did to Anton and Gemma, if the police got involved and that came out too . . .'

'You'd get away with it. They wouldn't be able to look at a face like yours and put you in jail . . .'

'What, a face covered in cuts and scars, you mean?'

'Oh yeah, you have a point there.'

We both laughed. But I'd started thinking about Anton and Gemma again and, of course, Jack noticed right away that I'd gone quiet.

'You OK?' he asked softly.

'I'm losing everyone, Jack. You're the only one left who doesn't hate me.' I knew I was wallowing but I couldn't help it.

'They don't hate you – no one could hate you. They're just confused because they don't know what's happening, that's all. We just have to find a way to show them. And we will. I promise.' I didn't know how he did it but he could always make me feel better. 'I saw you with your friends before this all got so out of hand, and I could see how they feel about you. They see all the same things I see: your passion, your talent, your humour and strength. That doesn't all go away overnight. You'll get them back when this is all over.' It was too much of a compliment for me to take. I couldn't understand how he really believed all that.

'I don't know where you get this stuff from Jack,' I laughed.

'I hope you're not going to try to argue with me, because you won't win.' I could hear the grin in his voice and picturing it made me long to see him.

'Will you be at the theatre tomorrow, if I'm early?' I asked, wishing I didn't have to wait even that long.

'I'm always there,' he answered with a little laugh. It was true.

'Don't you get tired of it?'

'Sometimes I wish I could do more, you know, be other places, have a life. But I do love it. The magic. You can create new worlds that live and breathe and unfold in front of you. You know?'

'Yes, I do.' I wondered just how exactly the same we felt. 'Do you ever want to act? To actually be *in* that different world?'

'I don't think I have the talent for it. I don't think I could deal with creating all those different emotions. I couldn't separate it from life, they'd spill over.'

'But it's a great way to let out the emotions you have already. You can channel them and vent them, and come away feeling calmer.'

'Is that how it works for you? I can't imagine having that much control over it – whereas with set-dressing and lighting, you have complete control. You don't just feel like you're *in* that different world, you feel like you're *creating* it and controlling it. You basically get to feel like God.'

'Ahh, I see, *now* I think I'm getting a better idea of how your mind works . . .' I laughed.

There was a silence for a moment.

'Hello?' I couldn't hear anything. 'Jack?'

'Hello?' There he was.

'What was that?' I asked.

'Sorry, I'm running out. Of money. I don't have long left. I should go really, anyway, it's late.'

I sighed. I didn't care how late it was, I could have talked all night.

'You *have* to move out of that place – or at least get a *mobile* . . .' I felt bad as soon as I'd said it, I didn't realise I'd sound like such a nag.

'I wish I could but, honestly, it's not possible. The digs sort of come with the apprenticeship so I don't exactly get to choose, and the free rent is instead of getting paid, so I have no . . .' There was another blank silence for a second. ' . . . seriously, not one single penny. Anyway, I'm going to let you go to sleep. The sooner you do, the sooner it'll be tomorrow. Come and see me as soon as you're up. Early as you like.'

'OK.' I smiled broadly at the thought. 'Goodnight.'

'Goodnight.'

Chapter 17

Bright sunshine streamed through my window as I woke up in the morning. I'd forgotten to close my curtains and a big angular patch of light was thrown across the floor and the bottom half of my bed. It was warm, even hot to the touch. Something dawned on me.

I remembered the porch light last night. It was the light that had brought me back!

What I didn't understand was how. There were lights around all the time – especially in the theatre. I needed to think this through because, if I could figure out how this worked, I might finally be able to take control.

The first time Olivia got me, it was the bright sunshine outside the theatre that brought me back – it wasn't leaving the theatre that had done it. I'd been standing in the cool of the darkened foyer, and when I stepped outside, the sunshine was too bright. It was the same the second time, when the bedside lamp had brought me back. I'd been in the dark bedroom for what seemed like ages and my eyes had got used to the dark. It was that flinch of light rushing into open pupils. That was what was shocking Olivia out of me. Last night had proved it – after walking through the fields, the flash of that security light was what got rid of her. There *was* a pattern.

One more practice left before opening night and I finally had a plan!

I got up and rushed through a shower so I could get straight to the theatre. It struck me how strange it was that I was so drawn to go back there, when Olivia was there, waiting. She'd made me turn away my friends and family and she'd left me broken. The whole theatre was full of bad memories and sick feelings and anger. But Jack was there too, and it was like I had an actual, physical ache to be near him.

I closed my eyes and painted his face in my mind. He was so soft and so strong all at once, with his messy dark hair, big, intense eyes and his broad jaw. His wide mouth and full lips with a cupid's bow . . . I suddenly realised maybe I didn't need to be in such a rush – I could take a bit of time over my hair and try to get it straight, maybe put some make-up on and find something nice to wear . . .

But Jack wasn't in the auditorium when I got to the theatre. I looked backstage, even in the props room where

I'd seen Olivia that time – and I really didn't want to go in there – but there was no sign of him. I even tried to go up to the lighting box, but it was locked. I almost gave up. I felt pretty stupid for putting all that effort into getting ready. I looked down at myself and suddenly felt embarrassingly overdressed.

It wasn't until I went up on stage that I found him. He didn't see me. He was in the wings on the opposite side, just standing over a control desk, staring. There was a notepad and pen beside him but he wasn't writing anything down. I felt an electric rush, just to see him standing there.

'Jack, what are you doing?' He almost literally jumped and I couldn't help laughing. 'Sorry! Did I scare you?'

'Yep.' He nodded, turned to face me and smiled. 'It's so good to see you're OK. Wow, you look . . . really, really good.'

I felt the blush heat my face. 'Thanks,' I smiled.

He walked towards me and I imagined him coming right up to me and reaching out to wrap me in his arms. I desperately wanted him to, with my whole being. But, of course, he stopped in his tracks before he'd got within reach. I reeled inside from not understanding. Did he think it would be ungentlemanly to touch me or something? He was so open on the phone and said such lovely things . . . I wondered if I should just make the first move – I didn't know how long it would be before I couldn't stop myself – but something always did stop me.

My chest felt so heavy I thought I might drop through the floor. It felt as if he didn't want me. How was I ever going to find out what was going on in his head?

I tried to claw back some of the excitement I'd felt about my plan. I clapped my hands together to try to snap myself out of it and I had to focus hard, but it sort of worked.

'Listen,' I rushed, 'I have to tell you about my plan. I've got an idea for today's rehearsal and I need your help.'

Jack nodded eagerly.

'Whenever Olivia takes me over, I always come back the same way – bright light. The first time, it was coming out of the theatre into bright sunshine, then it was turning on my bedside lamp . . . Last night it was the automatic light in the porch when my dad came home.' My excitement was coming back now. 'All we have to do is wait until she gets me this time, and then you can turn on whichever light is pointing in her direction – and it'll push her out again!'

I guess I was all wrapped up in thinking about me, because I was sort of expecting Jack to be as excited as I was. But he didn't look happy that we'd found the answer to getting rid of Olivia, he just looked worried. He turned and sat down on the front of the stage. I perched next to him, waiting for him to explain what was so wrong.

'I don't get it . . . If light brings you back, why haven't the stage lights brought you back before?'

'It has to be a shock – you know, when it's a sudden flash of light and your eyes squint. The lighting in our play

153

isn't like *The Wizard of Oz*. There aren't any effects. Every scene is in a room in the house, so the lighting is quite low really, and it's constant. And there are no monologues so even the spotlight's soft, and on all the way through. Your eyes don't get a chance to get used to the dark . . .' I realised as I was saying it what Jack's next objection would be.

'So how are we going to make it work then, if there are lights on all the way through?'

'In act four,' I explained. 'When Tristan and Diana think Rebecca's dead. They take her down to the cellar and cover the body. We'll have to wait until then. When the scene ends and Olivia comes out from under the throw, she'll be more sensitive to the lights. If you can get a second spot ready, as bright as you can get it, and flash it on, as if it was just a mistake . . .'

'I don't know, Zoë, it might not work unless she's looking directly at the lens when it comes on. That's if I can get my hands on the controls – I told you what Roger's like? He's a perfectionist, I can't even put my hands on the desk . . . I can't bear the thought of you letting her take you over again when you're relying on me to stop her. What if I can't do it?'

It hadn't occurred to me that he wouldn't be able to get to the controls. This Roger guy sounded like an absolute arse. And Jack had a point, I hadn't thought once that my plan might not work, but it was probably down to chance whether Olivia fell into the trap.

'I'm sorry, Jack, I hadn't thought about what I was asking you to do. If you think you'd get into trouble, we'll have to think of something else.'

'I'm not worried about that – honestly, you're more important than a job. I'm just terrified I won't be able to step in at the right moment – you'll be stuck with her . . .'

I loved that he was worried about me, but I didn't understand why he thought it would be so difficult.

'Don't worry so much. Listen, I've dealt with being stuck with her before and she hasn't killed me yet, just cuts and bruises.' I smiled. 'Once we get to the performance, I wouldn't want to be passing out on stage in the middle of a scene anyway – I'd rather let Olivia finish the play than have that happen and ruin it for everyone, but I need to see if this works. Just do your best, please? If it doesn't work, just sneak a torch from the caretaker's cupboard and follow me round with it till you get a chance to flash it in my eyes!' Joking didn't seem to calm his nerves.

'Of course I'll do everything I can – I just don't trust myself with the responsibility.'

'I trust you,' I said, putting a hand out to touch his, to comfort him. He pulled away like lightning and I swear it was like someone had stabbed me. It was so hurtful, such a blatant rejection, that I felt tears welling up and had to swallow hard and clench my jaw to keep from crying. What the hell was the matter with him? I couldn't keep quiet about it any more.

'Why do you always pull away . . .?'

'I'm so sorry,' Jack said before I could finish my sentence. When I looked at him he seemed genuinely as upset as I was. His voice was just a cracked whisper. 'I'm really so sorry, I didn't mean to.'

Something suddenly occurred to me. 'Do you have a girlfriend?' I asked, not wanting to know the answer.

His eyes widened with a sort of puppy-dog sadness and surprise. 'No, no. No, of course not . . . I wish I could explain it . . .' I wished he'd said yes, because it meant it must be me then, something wrong with me.

'It's OK,' I tried to say, without my voice cracking, 'you just don't feel that way. It's fine.' I was trying to be calm but I felt like I was shaking.

'No! That's not it either. I do. I *do* feel that way.'

I looked at him and finally couldn't keep the tears at bay any longer.

'I do,' he said. He said it looking into my eyes and I was so happy – but so confused. I just wanted him to hold me but he was already on his feet, ready to run away again. I looked away. I wanted him to know he was hurting me.

'I'm so sorry. I really am, if I could explain it, I – I wish I could tell you why but I just can't now. I'm sorry. I'll be in the lighting box watching, I promise.'

And then he was gone. Again.

All the way home I bit my lip and swallowed hard against the tears. There were five hours until rehearsal started and I spent most of it in my room, crying. It felt like I'd cried more in the last few weeks than I had in the last ten years combined. I felt so exhausted.

I hadn't heard from Steve since the last rehearsal and I knew it must be because he was too angry to speak to me. I knew he'd take me aside tonight and have another go at me. It'd be hard to see David too, after he made the effort to talk to me and I – Olivia – blanked him. On top of that, there was Jack – and all the other stupid guys in the world who played games with girls' hearts. I didn't know if I could take it.

'Why . . . Rebecca, darling . . . I thought you'd left over an hour ago. I . . .'

I was too tired to feel panic when Anton said that line at the rehearsal that evening. I felt hollow, like I'd used up all my emotion. The others looked through me instead of at me because of all the things I'd done to them. I was empty and invisible – it was like *I* was the ghost. Like Olivia had forced me into swapping places with her – it was like she was the one who was alive now, while I faded away.

She waited again, until the shooting, so I was lying down and couldn't run. I felt the familiar nausea and darkening vision and I thought of Jack. Despite how he confused me, somehow I still trusted he'd be watching out for me.

At the end of the scene, Olivia opened my eyes and

stood. She smoothed my top down with my palms and then looked out into the auditorium. There was a metallic clang and a spotlight shone right into my face. The rush made me smile before I blacked out.

You did it, Jack. Thank you.

'Have you talked to your dad about this?' Steve asked me as I sipped water, sitting on the chaise longue on stage. The others had gone for a break and instead of getting the grief from him I'd been prepared for, my collapse got me sympathy instead. I wished we'd worked the lights thing out sooner.

'I think you should,' he said when I shook my head.

'I don't think there's anything medically wrong with me. I think I'm just stressed out,' I argued.

'If you're suffering physical effects of stress as severe as passing out then that *is* something medically wrong,' Steve replied. 'If you're this ill, I don't know if you should be performing tomorrow . . .'

'*Please* don't say that, Steve.' I felt panic then – I couldn't go through all this and then get chucked out of the play just for fainting, surely? 'I've been trying so hard to keep on, despite everything – I mean, despite feeling stressed – because it's so important to me. It's only five performances – I can get through it, honestly. Please?'

'Well, let's see how you go through the rest of this evening, if you're sure you want to carry on?'

I nodded.

'But I'll have to speak to your dad about this before I can give you the go-ahead.'

He called Dad right then and told me afterwards that Dad was going to come and collect me. The rest of rehearsal was great and by the end, Dad was waiting at the back of the auditorium. There was no sign of another visit from Olivia and I finally got to do the end of the play myself. Me as me as Rebecca, not Olivia as me as Rebecca. I even got a wink from Steve at the end, which I think meant I did good and that he was happy to let me go on stage for the performances as long as Dad was.

As the others left, I deliberately dawdled so I could go and thank Jack. As Dad and I went to leave, I pretended I'd left my phone behind and came back in to find him. I went up to the lighting box. I rushed up the stair, took the handle and pushed – but the door wouldn't open.

Jack must have rushed to turn everything off and lock up before I could find him. Hurt and confused, I turned back as quickly and quietly as I could. I checked backstage again but there was no sign of him. In the end, I couldn't stall any longer and had to get in the car with Dad.

'I'm fine, honestly, Dad. I just forgot to eat or drink any water, and it was hot in there . . .' I argued with him in the car that we didn't need to go straight to a doctor. He looked sceptical and stern. 'Please can we just wait and see? I'll be extra careful and I promise if it happens again, I'll go.'

We were coming through the front door and I hoped the vague stains left in the carpet wouldn't remind Dad of the fainting I'd confessed to before.

'It's not right, Zo, there could be something really wrong . . .' he said.

I made my most pathetic pleading face and he relented a bit.

'OK, look, I'll just ring the doctors and see what they say. If they say you should go in, then I'm going to book you in, all right?'

I nodded reluctantly.

I couldn't sleep that night. My head was spinning. I was worried and excited about the play, still a little high from outwitting Olivia again, still happy that Jack had saved me from her, but still confused and angry about the way he'd been this afternoon. He cared enough to risk his job saving me from Olivia, but not enough to face me and just tell the truth. I lay there in the dark, willing him to call, watching my phone and trying not to blink, hoping with each second that passed that it would light up with an incoming call.

Chapter 18

I rested my hand lightly on the heavy fabric of the curtain and listened to the people filling the auditorium. I hadn't heard or seen Jack since I'd confronted him about pulling away from me. I'd officially frightened him off, I decided, and I was working hard at being angry with him instead of longing for him. The collective murmuring of the growing crowd was loud enough to give me a fluttering twinge of stage fright. Our side of the curtain, backstage, the bustling was weirdly silent (except for a few people saying *shhh* quite loudly). I wished my growing anxiety was just down to plain old first-night nerves but I had more to worry about than just fluffing my lines . . .

At least it was only Wednesday and we weren't expecting a full house until the Friday. But Dad was here. Because of the fainting, he said he'd only let me go on if he came with me to every performance – so he got tickets for all of them and I agreed to meet him at intermission and go home if I wasn't feeling well. I'd agreed just to keep him happy, but it wasn't really a promise I could keep. By intermission I didn't know where – or even who – I might be.

No matter how hard I tried not to, I kept looking around for Jack. One second I was frustrated with him for being so cagey, the next with myself for scaring him off. On the phone we could talk like we'd known each other for ever, but being in the same space together seemed impossible. If he'd just explain what was going on with him, maybe we could get past it . . . Maybe he just didn't want to see me any more.

I checked I wasn't being watched. We were under instruction not to try and peek at the audience but I couldn't resist. I wouldn't normally give in and break the rules, but Jack had exhausted my willpower and this seemed so unimportant I let myself look. I was so on edge I couldn't stay still or concentrate.

It was so crowded! Steve said they hadn't even nearly sold out but I wondered if he'd been lying to stop us getting nervous – I could only see about ten or so empty seats and people were still coming in. The lights were pretty low, but no lower than backstage, so I could see everyone quite clearly. I scanned the rows and spotted Dad. I kept looking, staring at the figures in black, wondering if maybe

162

Jack had been put on usher duty . . .

Then something drew my eyes a couple of rows back from Dad's seat. There was an immaculately-dressed old woman with a tiny, heart-shaped face . . . and a beautiful bright white shock of curls. I stopped breathing. I recognised that hair. And those delicate features were lined with age but I recognised them too. *Marion*.

There was no mistaking her from the photograph I'd seen. She looked serious, angry even, and my mind started racing. Why was she here? Maybe she'd just seen the posters up around town and came out of curiosity. No, she must be here because of the letter. I scanned the rest of the room, the side aisles and around the double doors at the back, looking for police uniforms. Nothing. Yet. Then an even worse thought struck me – if she hadn't called the police, maybe that meant she was planning to take the matter into her own hands. What if she was here to silence the new witness to her murderous plot from all those years ago?

I stared at her. She was eerily still in the hubbub. She was peering up at the stage. Her eyes moved slowly towards me and fixed – could she see me? I wanted to move but I was frozen still. She suddenly lifted her clutch bag, a beautiful, old-fashioned beaded thing, and searched through its contents. She nodded a tiny nod as she found what she was looking for, but she took nothing out. She rested the bag back on her lap, giving it a little pat, and smiled a satisfied smile. Oh God. Was it a gun? Did she have a gun in there? Should I make a run for it now? Panic rushed through me and gave me the power to move. I backed away from the curtain. If I ran now, I could get a pretty good head start while the first two plays were on . . .

I sneaked out to the green room to find my bag. Steve had put it in a big pile with all our stuff together – and there he was, guarding it, arms crossed, lips pursed. He looked at me with beady-eyed suspicion and insisted I sat with him. It was almost like he didn't trust me. Anyone would think I had a history of running out in the middle of rehearsals or something crazy like that. I thought about going to the ladies', but I knew Steve wasn't the type to be squeamish about following me in. I guess there'd be no easy escape for me.

At least the theatre was a public place, lots of people around to discourage murderers from their work. If Marion did anything to me in public, it would defeat the whole purpose of her coming here to silence me. I just had to keep away from her, that was all.

Finally, under Steve's ceaseless supervision, *Foul Play* was about to start. Anton and I sat at our act-one breakfast table as the curtain went up. I felt the heat of two hundred pairs of eyes boring into me and my heart was trying to beat its way out of my chest. But I held it together and, after we'd gone through a couple of lines each, it got easier. Actually, we were good.

Gemma and Anton were great, and watching them in their full costume and make-up, for a moment, I forgot everything, just letting myself get sucked into the play. But there was an empty space where Jack should have been. I wondered if he was in the lighting box, watching over me. Even as sure as I felt that he would be, it wasn't the same as having him there, smiling at me, making me feel like everything was all right.

But when I looked into the darkness of the wings opposite, only David was there, his eyes fixed on the stage. I wanted to try to sneak to the front and see what Marion was doing. I wanted to check she was sitting safely in her seat. Steve was still watching me like a hawk but I wasn't going to run away, not now.

Then Anton said that first line of act three. I wished I hadn't told Jack I didn't want him to try the lighting trick during a performance. Now that the moment was drawing closer, I felt physical revulsion at the thought of Olivia taking hold of me. I felt the fight in me coming back – I didn't want her to take over now. I was having too much fun. But she knew she had me trapped. She knew the way I felt about the play meant I wouldn't even try to resist her. Before I got to my first line, I was spinning and sick again, disappearing into the darkness.

Olivia was really good in the last act, but the injustice of it was tearing at me deep inside while she used me. I wanted to be free. As the audience clapped and cheered and we took our bows, I wanted to be me and have all my senses so I could soak up the moment. But I understood why Olivia wanted it, too. I wondered if part of her struggle to come back from the dead was just about being back here, reliving the life that had been stolen from her. But this was *my* life, not hers. Just because someone took her life from her didn't mean she got to have mine. It wasn't my fault.

We all filed off stage finally, but instead of going to the green room with the others, Olivia took me out into the auditorium. She fell into step with the crowds and was carried out into the foyer in the stream of people going for drinks. Inside Olivia's prison, the clamour of people's chatter and the clinking from the café sounded muffled and confused to me. I was helpless and paralysed again, not knowing where she would take me. Would I miss Dad? He'd be worried if he couldn't find me. But maybe that was better than if he did find me and Olivia said something evil to him. All I could do was wait and see what happened next.

I caught sight of Dad over by the exit, but his back was turned – and Olivia kept moving, she was looking for something, scanning the great room with my eyes. They stopped as they registered a shock of white curls . . .

She went straight for Marion then, and reached out with my hand just as Marion was turning towards us, grabbing her arm, hard. I saw her wince with fright as my fingers clamped viciously round her thin arm.

'You won't get away with murder, Marion, I know what you and Tom did. You're MURDERERS!' Olivia hissed. I was terrified of what she might do. 'You don't kill someone in front of all those people and get away with it. I might not have been able to find the gun or the evidence but I promise you you'll regret it if you don't give yourself up. You'll go to the police, now, and hand yourself in. Do you understand?'

Marion was stunned, frozen motionless.

Olivia tightened her grip. 'I'm warning you – I won't rest until you pay.' I could see the terror in Marion's eyes and I couldn't believe I'd been so scared of her. Everything about her seemed gentle. I felt terrible to be part of this attack.

'I thought it was an accident!' Marion cried. She seemed to sway on her feet. I could see she was shocked and confused about how I could know what I knew. It was like one part of her understood right away that it was Olivia talking through me, while another part struggled against accepting it, because it was crazy and impossible that some young girl she'd never met before could be having this conversation with her. 'It wasn't until Richard died and we cleared out his things that I found out the truth. And then I thought, it was so long ago, why dredge up the past and drag a dead man's name through the mud? He was my brother . . .' She was incredulous and pleading at the same time, but she didn't seem like a guilty killer – and I could sense Olivia was thrown by her openness.

'What are you talking about?' Olivia snapped at her, using my voice in a way I'd never used it – so hard and bitter. 'What does it have to do with *Richard*? You stole Tom from me, and then you both plotted to kill me by switching the gun. The police knew it, they just couldn't prove it. But now you're going to confess.'

Olivia let go of her arm, throwing it back at her, and I thought Marion might cry as she rubbed where my fingers had been digging in – her face was so full of hurt and disbelief.

'No, *no*. Olivia, Tom would never have cheated on you. I thought you *knew* that.' Her voice was small and wavering but beseeching – and amazingly compassionate, considering Olivia's violent tone. 'That was a lie Richard was trying to get you to believe, so he could be there to comfort you and steal you away from Tom. He was in love with you right from the start. I thought you knew, I thought you'd *know* he was lying.'

I felt so weird then – I could feel Olivia's shock and distress, my chest tightened with her sadness as she clutched at her heart with my hands. Then I felt her weaken – like she was loosening her grip on me. It even seemed like some of the darkness lifted. I saw my chance and I tried with all my strength to speak. I managed to make the tiniest squeak. It felt like a triumph but Marion barely noticed.

'Tom and I both believed it had been a genuine tragic accident, a mistake.' Marion shook her head. She reached out and took hold of my hand and looked into my eyes. 'He was devastated, Olivia. Broken. He never got over it really; he sort of wasted away in the end, with the drinking . . . I thought you *knew* . . . Oh.' She let go of my hand and her expression changed, as if she was seeing me for the first time, instead of seeing Olivia. 'I shouldn't be saying this to you, you're so young and you don't know me, but you're, well, Olivia, is almost the same age as I am, or at least she would be, if . . .'

Dad appeared behind Marion and helped her into a seat. He must have been watching – I guess we were causing a bit of a scene. I vaguely noticed an odd silence around us.

'Zoë, this is unbelievable – *unacceptable*!' Dad said fiercely under his breath. 'What are you doing upsetting this woman with —'

'No, please.' Marion interrupted Dad's rebuke with a soft touch of his arm and turned back to me.

'Olivia, or Zoë, is it? I found out after Richard, my brother, the director, died, that he'd become enraged that Olivia wasn't interested in him, even after all his efforts. There were notes and photographs and unposted letters in his things – I think he . . . wasn't in his right mind in the end.' She shook her head and looked away for a second. It must have been hard for her to say this about her own brother. 'In one letter, he wrote that if *he* couldn't have her, no one would.' She started to cry. 'That's when I knew it hadn't been an accident at all. He must have decided to swap the gun. Oh Olivia, don't you see? It was deliberate that he wanted it to look like it was Tom that shot you . . . and when we realised, it was too late . . .' It seemed like Marion was losing her senses then, reliving that awful night. 'The only person who'd guessed Richard's plan was that poor technician, but he couldn't stop it either. He tried to rush on stage before we got to that part of the scene but Richard held him back. He was bigger and stronger. So Richard had two deaths on his hands. I'm sure he didn't mean to kill the boy, but they must have struggled and I suppose he fell, and that would have been when he hit his head . . . but nobody knew while it was happening, you see, because on stage you were bleeding and . . . oh, he was such a nice boy, too, Jack – he tried to save you, you know, but Richard was so *angry* . . .'

Jack? She said Jack? I tried to shout – to push through Olivia's weakening hold – and it worked too – it came out as a whisper, but I had control again, I had a hold on my voice.

'The technician? You mean Christopher, don't you? Christopher John Bloom. That's what they called him in the newspaper.'

'No. Well, yes, I think his first name *was* Christopher, but everyone called him Jack, remember? Short for John? They said he fell over, but it was Richard that pushed him . . . I'm so sorry I didn't tell anyone when I found out but I was so *ashamed* . . .'

I swayed. I was spinning and dizzy. This couldn't be. Since when was *Jack* short for *John*? It didn't make any sense. She *couldn't* mean *my* Jack?

But then he was there, right in front of me, standing with his hand on his heart, his wonderful eyes full of sadness.

I reached out to him. It took all my effort moving that arm. Olivia was still clinging on, but she was getting weaker every second. Both our hearts were breaking.

Jack reached out too, but as our fingers met, they just went through each other. All I felt was the slightest chill. Tears ran down my face.

He was disappearing. He was actually fading right in front of me like a shadow when the sun goes in. Then he was gone. Pain and confusion tore through me. I barely heard what Marion was saying.

'Olivia, I'm so sorry, all those years,' she cried. I don't know if it was me or Olivia that turned my head to look at her. 'I wondered about the afterlife, you know, and if you were still out there, or up there somewhere, but whenever I pictured you, I always imagined you knew how much Tom loved you. You mustn't ever doubt that. I'll go to the police about Richard, I promise. I still have all the letters . . .'

Then I passed out.

Chapter 19

'Can you stand, sweetpea?' Dad whispered. He was on the floor with me, holding me in his arms. I opened my eyes and he helped me sit up. I could see Marion standing over me too, looking as shaky as I felt.

I wasn't sure about the answer to the question, but I gave it a try while Dad stopped me from falling.

'I think I'd better take my daughter home,' Dad said to Marion. 'Can I offer you a lift? Perhaps you'd like to come home with us? I'll make some tea?'

'Yes, that would be wonderful. Thank you.'

Marion helped Dad hold me up and we walked across the foyer to the doors. I was aware enough of what was happening to know everyone was watching, some of them were really staring, unashamedly open-mouthed. As we got close enough to the doors for me to feel the night air, people's whispers and exclamations were only just beginning to pierce the silence. I didn't care. I was filled with the image of Jack, fading away right in front of me. I couldn't believe it was true. Someone had to explain this to me. Until I could understand, I was in a numb limbo, like I was anaesthetised. I think our car ride home was silent. But I wonder if I would have heard it if either of them had said anything.

While Dad made tea and talked with Marion in the kitchen, I changed into my pyjamas and clawed my way back to consciousness. The more I allowed my senses to come back, the more I felt the creeping pain that came with beginning to understand what had happened that evening. I was glad Marion had come back with us. I needed her. There was no way I could explain to Dad without her.

We all sat together in the living room, hugging our cups with our hands as if it weren't a perfectly warm August evening. It was shock in our fingers, not cold. Gradually, together, Marion and I told Dad Olivia's story. And then I told *my* story – everything I could think of that had happened since that first possession at the theatre. By the time I'd finished, Marion was sitting next to me with an arm around me. I'd said sorry for the note I'd put through her door and she'd told me not to give it another thought. She'd just moved over beside me and held on to me.

Dad was holding his head in his hands, tufts of his fluffy hair sticking up between his fingers. When he looked up there were tears in his eyes.

'Why didn't you tell me any of this? You didn't have to go through it all alone.'

'How could I tell you, Dad? You wouldn't have believed it. I hardly believed it and it was *happening* to me.'

He shook his head like he just didn't have any words to say. We both knew I was right. Even with the whole story spilled out in front of him I knew a part of him thought it was all madness.

'Zoë?' Marion sat up as if she'd just thought of something and asked a question she seemed a little afraid to ask: 'Is Olivia still here? Can I speak to her again?'

For a few seconds I wondered if I knew the answer to that question. I felt my fingers, still clutching my cup, and my feet, curled up on the sofa, and they felt like mine again. Just mine. I hadn't felt like that since it all started. I shook my head.

'No,' I said to Marion. 'She's gone now.' And the second I said it I knew it was true, but as much as relief flooded through me, I knew what it meant. Jack was gone too. I started to cry. I can't describe the feeling of emptiness, except to say it felt like my soul had been torn out from inside me. 'I'm sorry.' I tried not to choke on the words.

'Not at all, dear. I think perhaps it's time for me to head home. Thank you so much for the tea, Mr Nelson.'

'No problem at all,' Dad said, as they both stood up and started fussing and organising the way older people do to try and avoid emotional scenes. 'I'd offer to drive you

174

home, but I think perhaps I should stay here – I could call you a cab?' I knew Dad wanted to stay for my sake so I interrupted as quickly as I could, concentrating hard on forming the words.

'Don't worry about me, Dad; drive Marion home. A few minutes alone would be good actually. I'll be fine.'

'OK, sweetpea, if you're sure?'

I nodded and waved Marion goodbye.

The door slammed and I sat alone, staring into the tepid dregs of my tea, thinking of Jack. I closed my eyes and pieced together all my memories of him bit by bit, right from the beginning. I realised I hadn't seen him until that first day on stage when Olivia first took hold of me. It was like the part of her in me was what had allowed me to see him. For all the horror and the hurt she'd caused me – she'd given me Jack too.

I thought about all the times we'd talked and how amazing it had felt – until I'd see him, and then he didn't seem to want to be seen with me. I'd taken it as a snub – but it was because he knew I'd look crazy, talking to someone no one else could see!

It made me shiver to think of it, but it wasn't from fear – it was like I wasn't just losing Jack but I was losing my memories of him too, because it hadn't been real, he hadn't really been there. But it *had* been real. Maybe not to anyone else, but to me it was.

It was all too much to try and take in. All the times I'd felt his rejection like a knife slicing through me – because he'd backed away from me when I tried to get close. I'd been sure it was a sign he didn't like me. But maybe it was because we *couldn't* touch, and if we'd tried I would have known. And I realised that every time I was hurting because of it, he'd been hurting too. Why couldn't he have told me? Had he worried about my reaction? Would I have stopped being able to see him if I'd known? Is that why he disappeared when I knew he was ... dead?

I ached inside thinking of it. I ached for what I hadn't known, for what he hadn't been able to tell me. And still, I ached to touch him, even now, knowing it was impossible.

I don't remember going to sleep, but I woke up suddenly, confused, a shrill ringing in my ear. It took me a second or two to work out what was going on. Then I knew. I don't remember consciously moving, I just remember the phone was in my hand in an instant.

'Jack?' I whispered, barely able to summon the breath to speak.

'Yes,' he whispered back. I sobbed silently with relief.

'I'm sorry,' he whispered. 'I couldn't tell you. I never meant to hurt you. But you'll be OK now. I love you, Zoë. Goodbye.'

'No! Please don't . . .' I gasped. I couldn't breathe, the pain in my chest . . .

Then the line was dead.

Chapter 20

'Wake up, Zoë.' Dad woke me gently the morning. 'I've made you a nine-twenty appointment with the doctor so I need you to get up, OK? I'm going to sit here till you're up,' he warned, knowing the old me would have gone back to sleep as soon as he left the room. But that was in another lifetime. 'I brought you some tea.'

It took me a few minutes to come round. My ribs hurt from sobbing myself to sleep. The more awake I got, the more I wished I wasn't. I didn't want to be awake and I definitely didn't want to go to the doctor.

Dad stuck to his word. We sat in silence as I sipped my tea.

'How are you feeling today?' he asked eventually.

'Pretty bad. But it's not anything the doctor can fix.' I looked at him pointedly.

'You're going to the doctor, young lady,' he said, more than matching my stubbornness.

'You don't believe me, do you?' I whined. 'After *all that* last night, you think I'm making it up – or I'm mad. That's why you want me to go to the doctor.'

'Oh, Zo,' Dad sighed a frustrated sigh. 'It's *so* hard. I never believed in all that stuff. I'm having to change the whole way I think about a lot of things all at once. But look, you're right, I saw the evidence right in front of me and, of course, I don't think you'd make something like this up. Please just give me a bit of time, OK? In the meantime, though, regardless of what the reason is that this has all been happening to you, your body's been through an awful lot. Look.'

He picked up my hands and stroked them better, like I was a little girl again.

'You're covered in grazes and scratches, you've been fainting and your sleep's been disturbed . . .' Oh, he'd noticed that . . . I guess the walls in our house *are* pretty thin. 'I just want her to check you over and tell me you're OK. OK?'

I tried to shower as quickly as I could so it didn't wake me up too much. I was happy to have that protective, numbing blanket of sleepiness to stop me feeling too much.

I hate the doctors' surgery. The waiting room is full of ill, infected people and you think with every breath you're going to catch some horrible lurgy. Everything's dank like

178

a rainy day, even in summer. All grey lino and brown plastic. I sent Dad for coffee and sat alone, waiting to be called, trying my hardest not to think of Jack, feeling like I could easily burst into tears at any minute if I didn't concentrate hard.

Of course I thought of him. I had so many questions and I knew that, as time went on, I'd just have more. How did he phone me? How did he turn the spotlight on that day? That night we'd both dreamed of each other, when he said we could pretend we'd had the same one, was there any chance . . . that it had been more than a dream?

There was one question I knew the answer to, though. I knew he loved me. He couldn't save Olivia but he'd saved me. He'd said I'd be all right now. He'd said he loved me.

The little intercom speaker crackled and the doctor called my name from her office. I hate going into that little interview room. I feel like I'm on trial – and it reminds me of French oral exams. Only with poking and prodding and cold metal instruments.

'I'm fine,' I told the doctor before I told her what Dad wanted me to tell her. I didn't tell her the whole truth, but I did tell her I'd passed out. I also told her a couple more times that I was nevertheless fine.

'Passing out isn't normal if you're fine,' she said firmly to me. She asked me lots of questions and finally, after she'd weighed me, squidged my eyelids about, used some instruments on me and shone various lights into various places, she sighed. 'You're sure there's nothing you haven't told me?'

I nodded.

'Then I won't send you straight to hospital. The weather's been hot and it sounds like you've been busy with things and haven't been concentrating on looking after yourself. But I want you to go for some tests over the next couple of weeks – the hospital will call you when they can fit you in – and I want you to take it a bit easier for a while. *And* – I want you to come back straight away if you faint again, OK?'

I nodded again and scuttled out of there as soon as I could get away.

I found Dad outside just finishing a phone call and balancing two lattes in one hand. I told him I was fine. He squinted suspiciously at me.

'*Honestly*,' I said. 'Stop worrying.'

He said he'd just finished speaking to Steve. 'I told him you might not be up to the performance tonight. He's looking into taking the play off the programme, just for tonight, and he doesn't think it'll be a problem. So you don't have to go if you don't want to – OK? He said take a few hours, see how you feel, and let him know by four.'

'Thanks, Dad,' I said.

I didn't know what to do. I felt relieved knowing I could back out if I wanted. But a big part of me really wanted to go on with the play – I wanted to do it properly, doing all my acting myself. But I did feel odd about going back there so soon, with the memories of everything all stuck to the building like splatters of debris after an explosion. And I was tired – absolutely worn out. And I couldn't imagine what people would be thinking about me after that spectacle of insanity I'd put on. The thing is, weird as it seemed to me through the grief I was feeling, despite feeling more alone than ever, I felt calmer and more like myself than I had for a really long time, too.

'That's good to know,' I told him finally. 'I'll have a shower and chill out for a bit and see how I feel.'

We walked home without needing to speak, sipping our coffees.

I didn't hear the knock at the door, what with the hairdryer blasting, but when I'd finished I could hear voices in the hall. I opened my bedroom door and crept to the top of the stairs where I could peek down. It was David.

When Dad turned to call me I was already halfway down the stairs.

'Hey, how you doing?' David gave me a smile. I couldn't believe he'd actually come to my house to check I was OK.

'I'm OK, thanks. I think.'

'You up to going for a walk?'

I was slightly stunned. 'Sure, give me a sec, I'll grab my bag.' I raised my eyebrows briefly at Dad and he gave me a little nod. I felt a bit nervous about what David might say on our little stroll, but awful as the possibilities might be, there was no way I was going to miss the chance to be friends again, if that's what he was offering.

'So . . . There was all sorts of buzz and gossip after you left last night.' David got straight to the point the second the front door clicked shut behind us.

'Oh *God* . . .' was all I could say, although he smiled at me and I felt hopeful that this conversation might be OK.

'Some people actually thought it was part of the play.' He grinned, shaking his head. 'You know, one of those fancy "post-modern statements where the action spills off the stage".' David's impression of posh, hobnobbing theatre-goers made me laugh.

'Other people thought I was crazy, though, right? Or having some sort of breakdown?' I looked at David and he was honest enough to nod. He put a comforting arm round me and I thought of Jack. I was overwhelmed for a second and had to hold my breath to try to fight the tears. It was such a simple thing, putting your arm round someone. You did it without thinking. But Jack and I never had the chance. We never would.

'Oh man, don't cry. Damn, sorry. I said the wrong thing. I'm so bad at this.'

'No, no.' I touched his hand, which was still resting on my shoulder. 'You're not. Not at all. It's not you.' He smiled and put his hands back in his pockets as we kept walking.

'Steve says you're not sure you'll make it for the performance tonight . . . Obviously we get it, totally, if you can't but we'd love it if you would.'

'We?' I asked, my heart beating a bit faster.

'Yeah, Gemma and Anton and I all talked about it. I dunno, mate, this whole thing is properly insane-weird, you know. It messes with your head to even try to think of the explanation for it. But we all agreed we can at least try to forget it all, you know, get past it. They're waiting for us at the diner, if you feel like going – it'd be just like old times.'

Then I properly cried. I couldn't hold in my tears – they still cared enough to give me another chance.

'Not again! What are you like? Come here.' David gave me a proper hug then and it felt sort of like coming home. I let myself cry for a few seconds and then took a breath in and tried to pull myself together. I let go of David and wiped my face with my hands.

'You're sure? You're sure they mean it, after everything I did?'

'Well, you know, the whole violence thing left them a bit sore, but when you started beating up old ladies as well, they at least figured it wasn't anything personal.'

I laughed.

'Come on then, let's go say hi,' David said as he took my hand.

Other books in the Piccadilly Love Stories collection:

My Best Friend's Brother

Laura Ellen Kennedy

Erica is on cloud nine when she falls for Jake, Sally's older brother, and discovers he feels the same. But when Sally confides in her about a family secret, Erica finds herself in a terrible dilemma. She hates lying to Jake, but telling him would mean betraying Sally's trust. Either way, Erica risks losing her best friend or her boyfriend . . . or maybe both.

A heartrending story of love and friendship under pressure.

'Pulls you quickly in, poses a complicated problem, lets all the characters have their say and carries a real and raw emotional charge.'
School Librarian

HILARY FREEMAN

Naomi is restless. She's on her gap year and stuck at home with her parents while all her friends are travelling or away at university. Then she meets Danny, a mysterious and intense musician who opens her eyes to a whole new world around her. Danny is exciting and talented, and his band are on the brink of stardom. But he also has a dark, destructive side . . .

Will Naomi be able to save Danny before it's too late? And, more importantly, can she save herself?

'Warm, witty, compelling and insightful, it's a great read.'
Sunday Express

HILARY FREEMAN

Lily believes her boyfriend Jack is perfect, but wonders why he won't talk about his past. Wouldn't it be fantastic, she thinks, if she could talk to his ex and fill in all the gaps?

Lily devises a way to do just that. But what begins as a bit of fun has unexpected – and disturbing – consequences . . .

DON'T ASK is a story about love, friendship and secrets. Sometimes it's better not to ask too many questions.

'Completely riveting from start to finish . . . plenty of humour, alongside the slightly darker storyline. Thoroughly recommended!'
Chicklish

Things ☽
I Know
About
Love

KATE LE VANN

Things I know about love.
1. People don't always tell you the truth about how they feel.
2. Nothing that happens between two people is guaranteed to be private.
3. I don't know if you ever get over having your heart broken.

Livia's experience of love has been disappointing, to say the least. But all that is about to change. After years of illness, she's off to spend the summer with her brother in America. She's making up for lost time, and she's writing it all down in her private blog.

America is everything she'd dreamed of – and then she meets Adam. Can Livia put the past behind her and risk falling in love again?

'Compelling and compassionate.' *Carousel*
'Rawly honest, rich in humour.' *Books for Keeps*

☆

www.piccadillypress.co.uk

☆ The latest news on forthcoming books

☆ Chapter previews

☆ Author biographies

☆ Fun quizzes

☆ Reader reviews

☆ Competitions and fab prizes

☆ Book features and cool downloads

☆ And much, much more . . .

Log on and check it out!

Piccadilly Press

☆